BUTTER BEANS, BUTTERFLIES AND BUS RIDES

A collection of prose and poetry

The White Hill Writers

www.thewhitehillwriters.com

CONTENTS

ACKNOWLEDGEMENTS

The White Hill Writers

First of all, thanks must go to Linda Dawe who drew us all into her classes and set us on our journey to explore the written word. Her knowledge, wit, critical appraisal and encouragement provided the impetus to keep us welded together as we delved deeper into our imaginations during lockdown.

From within the group itself a special mention goes to Garry Giles for initiating the Zoom meetings and throwing out fresh writing challenges each week. Without his diligence and enthusiasm, we might not have grown together so effectively.

Various talents within the group have also directed and guided us to the final production of this work. We are grateful for all this shared knowledge and experience.

Book Cover

Many thanks to Damir Mijailovic (full cover butterfly wing abstract) and Richard Hounsfield (Chesham Memory Tree watercolour insert) for the cover artwork.

Chesham Memory Tree, White Hill

Overlooking Chesham is Dungrove Farm. In the middle of one of its fields is the locally-named 'Memory Tree', a huge sentry-like oak that stands alone and proud over the town, conveying an air of mysticism to all who view it. It is about 300 years old and is renowned as a site of ritual and spiritual symbolism, ceremonies and scattering of ashes in memory of friends and relatives. Visitors sit under its boughs for calm reflection and contemplation, with many attaching trinkets to its lower branches where the tree holds these dear memories aloft in the breeze.

This magnificent tree is emblematic of The White Hill Writers ambition to write stories about people and events, in our lifetimes and beyond.

INTRODUCTION

The White Hill Writers are a motley crew who came together at the White Hill Centre in Chesham. When the COVID pandemic put a stop to that, our love of writing continued to bind us together and we challenged ourselves to write from home, checking in weekly on Zoom to share ideas.

It not only provided a focus and escape from our lockdown situations but also engaged our minds effectively. Gradually, as we accumulated a substantial body of work, we felt encouraged to share it. So here we have pulled together a varied collection of prose and poetry embracing thoughtful reflections and celebrating the resilience of the imagination.

Included in the collection are pieces expressing our appreciation of the Chilterns which have provided an idyllic landscape, not only inspiring, but also sustaining us during a year of disruption and limitations.

This publication has taken us on an unexpected journey of perseverance, drawing upon hidden talents within the group while researching and gaining new skills along the way. So, we are proud to have arrived in this space.

Hopefully the book will bring pleasure. If any of the prose or poetry resonates or lifts your spirits that is an achievement for us; if you are tempted to explore the Chilterns that is a bonus. If it inspires you to write, well, that is simply wonderful.

We hope that you enjoy reading our contributions.

CHAPTER 1

SUSPENSE

The Prisoner

Sarah-Jane Reeve

O ne cold December night last year, Geoff and I were in the kitchen eating dinner when we heard a newsflash on the radio. Someone had escaped from the prison on the moors outside our town, only two miles from our house.

"Good grief!" said Geoff. "That's never happened before."

"I've always loved that our house backs onto the moor but that's only a walk from here," I said.

"It's only an open prison, I'm surprised it doesn't happen more often."

"They don't put anyone dangerous in there though, do they?" I said.

"I wouldn't be too sure..." Geoff took our plates to the sink.

I went to the kitchen window to see what was going on, but I couldn't see anything. Suddenly there was an urgent knocking at the front door. I nearly jumped out of my skin.

We looked at each other. The knocking started again, and then the doorbell rang.

"Wait a minute!" said Geoff. "We can't just open the door ... What if it's him? The escaped prisoner."

"Let's talk first," I said. "Hello!" I said loudly with my ear against the front door. "Who is it?"

"It's the police. PC Sally Walker. There's been an incident locally. No cause for alarm, but could I have a quick word?"

We both sighed with relief.

"OK!" said Geoff, opening the door.

On the doorstep was a smiling uniformed woman police officer wearing a hat, stab vest and carrying a clipboard.

"Good evening, sir and madam," she said, "I don't know if you've heard but a prisoner has escaped down the road at Riverdown Moor Prison. We're going house to house just asking if anyone has seen anything unusual."

"We've only just heard about it on the radio," said Geoff. "We haven't seen anything, have we Sue?"

"Nothing so far," I said. "We've only been looking out of the windows."

"Well," continued the PC, "we're just telling everyone. If you do see anything suspicious, just ring 999."

We nodded.

"The person concerned isn't known to be dangerous, but you never know when prisoners get desperate, so do stay inside. And, for those of you with houses looking out onto the moors, we're asking you to write down your phone numbers for us so we can contact you if necessary."

At this point she held out the clipboard she was carrying under her arm:

"Oh dear!" she said. "Silly me, I've left my pen in the car – you're the first house I've called at."

"Oh, I've got one here somewhere, if you'll come inside, Constable," Geoff said.

We ushered PC Sally into the hall, while we both dithered about searching for a pen, eventually uncovering one under the chaotic heap of papers on the desk in the corner: Geoff's teaching stuff, and my shop accounts. We're ridiculously untidy.

Geoff wrote down our address and number on the clipboard, handed it back to her and told her to keep the pen. By this time the PC's personal radio was crackling.

"Thank you. Well, they'll want me to check in and get back to it," said Sally. "And don't worry, we'll get the helicopter out soon, and it will all be over."

Geoff shivered.

"He's a right fool. Trying to escape in this weather, he'll give up soon enough."

The PC left and we heard a police siren in the distance. We locked and bolted the door.

"Goodness, she looked so young!" said Geoff.

"Yes! But they're so organised, aren't they? I feel quite protected, don't you?" I said, putting the kettle on.

Sure enough, as we got into bed we heard the sound of the helicopter scanning the moors. It went right over our house two or three times, and it was deafening, you couldn't hear yourself think. Thankfully after that it all went quiet. We listened to the midnight news but there were no further developments. We fell asleep.

We woke at 6.30 a.m. as usual to get ready for work. At around 7.15 Geoff was ready to go.

"I'm off early," said Geoff, "I've got the Year 10 mock GCSEs to organise, and a Year 7 assembly. OK if I have the car today?"

"Yes, I can cycle in," I said. "I might as well open the shop early." I got into the shower.

When I went downstairs, I found Geoff in the kitchen looking flustered.

"I thought you'd left," I said.

"I couldn't find the car keys. I had to get the spares from the desk drawer, then I went outside – and the car's gone! I looked to see if you'd parked it on the street but it's nowhere to be seen."

"What! I definitely parked it on the drive last night. I usually leave the keys on the hall bookcase near the front door…"

Suddenly, I got a sinking feeling.

"Oh Geoff, you don't think…?"

Just then, a newsflash came on the radio:

"Breaking news on the Riverdown Prisoner escape: the prisoner has been identified as Anita Sawyer, imprisoned seven years ago as an accessory to murder. She has assaulted a PC, Sally Walker, and stolen her uniform. She also has a history of car theft. Police think she may be planning to steal a vehicle. Members of the public are warned not to approach the prisoner."

Ahmed

Joyce Smith

Yasmeen ran down the path to get away from them, but who were they? Were they getting closer? She concentrated on listening to the sound of the gunshots. What direction were they coming from? In response to what she was hearing, she veered off to the left and made her way to one of many derelict buildings, standing like broken teeth down a rubble-strewn narrow street, silent and blind. She was trembling with fear. Were they army or rebels? It would probably not make much difference if they came across her. She did not want to think about that because she knew what had happened to others, caught out in the open on their own. She drew her shawl over her dark hair and across her face and prepared to wait until it was safe to leave.

She had been forced to leave the relative safety of a basement she shared with her family below a bombed building. Her father desperately needed medication and they were rapidly running out of food. Her two brothers, who usually brought them provisions, were fighting for one of the rebel groups and had not been home in three days. As the days went by, she feared for them. At fifteen years of age, she was very aware that the responsibility was now hers. Crouched down inside the building, grateful for the shade after the intense noonday heat, she listened for any approach. She caught a faint noise behind her. Turning around in alarm, she made out the shape of someone in a dark corner.

She froze, not daring to move, fearing the worst, when

she heard a soft sob of fear. Closer inspection revealed a young boy, no more than twelve or thirteen. She waited to see if he was on his own. Satisfied, she crawled across the open space and touched his arm. The boy flinched away from her. He was thin and dirty and obviously terrified. His dark eyes seemed too big for his face and the terror in them was evident.

"Please, help me," he whimpered. "I don't want to fight; they will make me fight."

"Where are your family?" Yasmeen asked gently.

Breaking out into fresh sobs, the boy said, "They are all dead. A bomb hit our house. I am the only one left."

The sound of gunfire was receding. Yasmeen had a choice to make. When the gunfire ceased, she took his arm.

"Come with me but keep very quiet," she said in a low voice.

The boy stopped snivelling and began to follow her. It seemed to take forever. They kept close to walls and scuttled from one patch of shade to another, climbing over large chunks of concrete, furniture and other pieces of people's lives, until they reached the basement where her family greeted her with great consternation.

"Who is this? Why are you taking such a risk? Are you mad?" demanded Amira, her mother, waving her hands and shaking her many bracelets.

Yasmeen quickly explained what had befallen Ahmed's family. It took a lot of persuading on her part but with much grumbling her parents had no choice but to allow him to stay.

"Just for now," they said. "We cannot afford to feed him, and we don't know if we can trust him."

In the next few weeks, however, he proved himself

invaluable. Of her brothers, Farid and Hassan, there was no sign. The family feared the worst. The brothers had no wish to be fighters, but it was hoped that they had been commandeered to fight in another area, because the alternative was far, far worse. Quick footed and intelligent, Ahmed took over the job of finding food for the family and seemed able to find places where shops had been bombed and their goods left unguarded. Over time her father, Jamal, began to deteriorate and without hospital treatment and medication, he quickly got worse. More and more he depended on Yasmeen and Ahmed to feed and guard them. One morning they realised he had given up the fight. They had to bury him late at night under a pile of stones.

At first, Yasmeen and Amira stayed in the basement with Ahmed's help. It was cramped and dark and they sometimes saw rats slithering between the fallen masonry. They were often hungry and cold when the temperature dropped in the Syrian night. They were, however, near a water supply, a broken pipe that dripped intermittently into a bowl they had salvaged from their ruined house. They managed to remain hidden and safe over the next few months, hoping against hope that hostilities would cease. Of Yasmeen's brothers, there was no sign. Over time Ahmed grew taller and broader and began to show signs of growing a beard. They feared he would be taken one day to fight. The day came when he did not return from a foraging trip.

The situation in the city was getting worse. Bombing went on at all hours, and the sound of gunshots filled the air from morning to night. Frightened and alone, Yasmeen and her mother decided they could no longer live in the dingy basement without support and decided they would try to make their way to the border, hoping to make for the relative safety of the Turkish camps. Though they feared what life might hold for them there, it was preferable to their precarious existence in Syria.

They gathered up their few belongings and some provisions they had managed to save for such an undertaking and left the safety of their basement. Yasmeen was tall for her age, and it was decided it would be safer if she dressed in some of her brother's clothes. The trousers were cinched in with a belt and the kaftan over the top was tied up with one of her mother's scarves. With a *gutrah*, a scarf-like head covering, pulled around her face, she could pass for a boy. They travelled at night along the side of the main highway despite the intense cold and the danger of discovery, flattening themselves on the ground when vehicles went past. During the day they hid in dry riverbeds or derelict buildings to avoid the relentless sun and capture. They passed burnt out vehicles and bomb craters: evidence of the devastating civil war that gripped their country. They were not the only ones trying to get to the border but kept themselves to themselves.

One night, agonisingly close to the border, they heard many vehicles and quickly hid from view behind some rocks. But instead of travelling on, the vehicles stopped. Yasmeen and her mother lay paralysed with fear, hoping against hope that they were shielded from view, when a young fighter stepped out in front of them. He stared at them with hard eyes for what seemed ages, until, lifting his hand, he signalled to his comrades that there was no one there. As he turned away, his face was visible in the moonlight. It was Ahmed.

The Clues

Garry Giles

In the later summer months, I love to have the windows open at night. The sounds from outside are wonderful. I can hear the muntjac deer nibbling, almost 'hoovering' up the acorns from the oak trees; the badgers 'snuffling' around as they do; and the occasional hoot from an owl. It is time for bed though.

Bed is a favourite place: that place of comfort, that place of warmth, and the sense of feeling safe. The place that just feels so special.

As usual I am reading a book, although I am somehow distracted, I do not really know why, but I have found myself reading this last paragraph at least three times. I wish I could work out what is on my mind.

I get up and tea is my solace. I am tempted by a ginger nut, oh and then another. Maybe I should go for a walk? Then I realise that it would just wake me up even more. I find the newspaper from last weekend and find the 'giant' general knowledge crossword. That will do.

Back in bed I am struggling a bit with it, though finding the link between 14 down and 23 across is oh so satisfying. I am tempted to 'Google' some of the answers but I decide to plough the furrows of my mind a bit further.

I hear the doorbell ring a couple of times, look at the clock and see that it is 1:30 in the morning. I have been asleep but I am sitting up and the newspaper and pen are laying before me, I must have been thinking about the clues in my sleep. But it rings again. Why would someone be ringing on my doorbell at this time? I look out of the window hoping that I do not see a police car, as that would undoubtably be bad news this early in the morning. There is nothing to be seen. But the doorbell still rings. I am loath to answer the door.

I creep down the stairs in the darkness so as not to be seen, though I can see that I am casting shadows from the light that is still on upstairs from when I was having a go at the crossword. Whoever it is must surely now know that I am around.

What do I do? Do I open the door, or do I just try and hide? I have made it down the steps of the stairs, all 14 of them but now I am scared. I am only a truly short distance from the person at the other side of my front door. I wish that I could see who it is.

I get on all fours and creep to the kitchen; I dare not turn on the light but now I do not know what to do. In addition to the doorbell there is now banging on the door. Who is doing this to me? And what do I do now?

I resolve to open the door, but I fumble in the dark to find my coat in the back room so that I feel as if I have some sort of protection. With my coat on I brace myself, turn the light on and get the key for the front door. Opening the door, I am shocked to find a tearful neighbour from number 23 across the road.

"Sorry to bother you this late but I have forgotten my keys and you have the only spare set."

"No problem," I say and get her keys and hand them over.

Closing the door and going back to bed I find it creepy that 14 (steps) down, and 23 across (the road) had occurred twice.

Kitchen Calamity

Lorraine Surridge

"Oh why, oh why did I come here?" Verity wailed.

This was supposed to be her chance to escape the trauma of the last year. A time to relax alone and concentrate on getting her life back on track. But she had been stuck in this remote cottage where it hadn't stopped raining for days. No chance to take those long walks across the moor or along the cliffs to help clear her head. Not even an opportunity to get out and replenish the rapidly diminishing supplies in the larder. Frankly, she had thought she would never hate pasta, but fusilli for every meal was becoming tedious.

The floods had cut off the access road to the cottage so, even if there had been a phone signal or an internet connection to order a food delivery, it was impossible for any delivery van to reach her. At least the oil-fired generator was still working so she had hot water and light. She also had plenty of dry logs stored under the porch for the log burner in the snug. However, none of that helped to relieve the stress she was feeling. Her nerves were on edge most of the time.

"For heaven's sake Verity, why didn't you listen to Mum and just book a fortnight at a swanky spa on the Riviera instead of a remote Cornish farm cottage?" she scolded herself as she popped upstairs to close the windows as the rain fell even harder than before.

She sighed heavily at the thought of the casement windows rattling all night if they had to be kept shut. As she dropped the last window latch, she heard what she thought was a distant echo of thunder. The rumble grew louder and louder until she was convinced there must be a juggernaut thundering towards the cottage. Verity stood frozen at the top of the stairs when there was an enormous boom from the kitchen followed by a rush of freezing cold air whooshing up the stairs. Shaking with shock she hesitantly descended the stairs, one step at a time. As she peered around the door into the kitchen, she couldn't believe what she saw. A huge hole had appeared in the kitchen floor.

"Oh God, a sinkhole!" she screamed just as all the lights went out.

In the darkness Verity stood stock still, scared and unable to move whilst fighting down an urge to run away. She could feel a blast of cold air coming up from the hole in the floor accompanied by the most horrendous stink, a mixture of seaweed and rotting fish. As her eyes adjusted to the darkness, she got her bearings from the light coming from the range cooker. Its amber glow helped her identify the whereabouts of her handbag which she kept hung over the chair next to the range. If she could just reach her bag, then she would be able to use the torch in her mobile phone to see her way safely out of the cottage.

Breathing heavily, but trying her best to keep calm, she stepped tentatively with crablike movements from the door to the cooker hoping the hole in the floor was not getting wider in the dark. After about eight steps she could feel the warmth of the cooker then suddenly the knuckles on her left hand struck the back of the chair. Verity felt for the strap of her handbag and lifting it off the chair she absentmindedly slung it over her shoulder as she if she was off to the shops. Unzipping the bag she ferreted about for her phone. The screen illuminated as soon as she pressed the 'on' button and, after three failed attempts, she finally tapped in the right pin number. As she switched on the torchlight the small kitchen lit up.

Reluctantly Verity edged closer to the sinkhole, and as she peered down into it, she instantly realised there was one thing wrong with her theory. A natural sinkhole would not have inbuilt steps hewn into the rock face of the hole.

Verity stood there undecided as to what to do next. The road away from the cottage was impassable but equally she felt it was too precarious to stay at the cottage where the hole had possibly made the structure unsafe. Feeling in her bag for her car keys she decided the best course of action was to go back upstairs and pack, then go outside and sit in her car ready to make a quick dash to safety when possible.

Finally, after an uncomfortable wait of three hours a pallid dove-grey dawn approached. The new day brought with it the clearest skies she had seen for several days. Perhaps a respite from the rain would allow the flood waters to recede, she pondered. As Verity sat in her car contemplating her options, she noticed with relief the welcome sight of a farm vehicle with huge wheels trundling towards the cottage.

Suddenly scared that the approaching heavy vehicle would trigger a further collapse of the tunnel Verity jumped out of her car and ran towards the oncoming vehicle waving frantically to the driver to stop.

The tractor came to a halt about 100 yards away from Verity. The cab door was flung open, and the driver shouted something to her which she found impossible to hear above the noise of the diesel engine.

As Verity reached the tractor she heard the man repeat, "Mum sent me to check on you. We own the holiday let.

Do you want a tow?"

He jumped down to the ground and stood in front of Verity.

"If your family owns the cottage you'd better come and look at this first," she replied.

With that said, Verity turned to walk towards the building assuming he would follow.

She was inside the cottage for about a minute before he hesitatingly came in behind her. Daylight now illuminated the devastation caused by the tunnel collapse.

"Blimey!" he exclaimed. "The old smuggler tunnel. It's said it leads right to the sea. Legend has it that a couple of hundred years ago smuggled goods were brought along the tunnel to this cottage, then teams of horses would follow pony trails to avoid the excise men by spiriting the contraband away in the dead of night across the moor. All these days of continuous rain must have washed away the soil exposing the cavern under the cottage."

Verity was no longer listening but was staring intently at his face. It was a nice face.

"You'd better grab your stuff and I'll take you back with me to our farm. I'm Jack, by the way," he said, holding out his hand.

"Verity," she replied in a trance, taking his hand and staring at Jack's impossibly long eyelashes.

"Do you need to collect your belongings?" she heard Jack say.

"It's all in the car," Verity replied.

"Let's get gone then." And with that, Jack led the way out of the cottage, leaving Verity to close the door behind them.

After moving her car closer to the tractor, Jack deftly attached a tow rope, joining the two vehicles together and then, making sure Verity was comfortable with driving on a tow rope, he set off slowly back towards their farm.

Twenty minutes later Verity was sitting in Jack's family's farmhouse kitchen. Over a cup of tea and while consuming the biggest slice of cake she had ever eaten, the family discussed the tale of the smugglers' tunnel.

"Thought it was just a Cornish legend," Jack's mum had said. "I can't believe we have had guests staying in a building that could collapse at any moment. Makes me feel quite faint."

Jack's grandpa was sitting in front of the fireplace when he announced, "It's all this rain."

"Yes, Gramps, we know, that's why the tunnel collapsed," Jack said loudly, indicating to Verity that his grandpa was hard of hearing.

Ignoring Jack, or possibly just being deaf to his grandson's comment, Grandpa continued, "It's called Smjuga for a reason."

"We know what the cottage is called, Gramps," Jack's Mum said kindly.

Verity remembered when she had booked to stay at Smjuga Cottage she had assumed it was a Cornish place name.

"Is it a named after a place in Cornwall?" she asked.

Grandpa turned to look intently at Verity and explained, "No, lass, it's where the word smuggle comes from. Smjuga is Norse. It means: 'to creep into a hole'."

"Well, I'm up for it," Verity announced.

Everyone turned to look quizzically at Verity.

"Up for what exactly?" Jack's mum asked.

"I'd like to creep into that hole and take a look. It would

be exciting to explore the past. You know you really have a great U.S.P. for your holiday cottage," Verity announced.

"You what?" Grandpa repeated.

Verity and Jack exchanged smiles.

"Unique Selling Point," explained Jack. Now with greater confidence, he announced: "Well, that's a great proposition and here's another one. Verity, how about you finish your holiday by staying here in our spare room and we could go exploring together… if you want to, that is?"

Jack was suddenly less sure of himself and wondered if he had overstepped the mark.

"I would be thrilled to," Verity replied.

Jack's mum looked on with confusion. *Well,* she thought to herself, *and I was pretty sure Jack was gay.*

Thinking along the same lines, Jack hadn't misread the expression in his mum's face. *Well, at least that will halt all the probing questions for a while,* Jack thought.

Addressing Verity, Jack said, "Great, we'll check the times for the high and low tides and I'll ask a mate of mine who does a bit of potholing to loan us some safety equipment."

Finding herself grateful after all that she hadn't taken a trip to the Riviera, Verity's mood lifted for the first time in several months as she found she actually had something to look forward to. And all because of a hole in the floor. *Maybe some clouds do have a silver lining,* she thought to herself.

The Intrusion

Moyra Zaman

Despite the dark morning, Marion woke early and was up and about well before dawn broke. Ever since her husband died seven years ago, she had rarely slept well at night. Today, however, she was glad to capture these hours of stillness and gain control of her thoughts before the bustle of family life took over. She needed to plan her day and make a list.

This was one of those rare occasions when all the family were united under one roof in the run up to Christmas. Her daughter Lorna, and her husband Gus, had come to join them from France, where they now lived. Her eldest son, Jamie, was back from Uni and the younger two, Mark and Lisa, who were still at home, were enjoying the temporary disruption; Lisa, especially, appreciated the opportunity to sleep in the attic while the heating was on there over the Christmas period.

Downstairs, Marion breathed a contented sigh, feeling fortunate to have her children around at this, often emotional, time of year. She grabbed a cup of tea and allowed her senses to tune in to the internal rumblings of her home, those familiar sounds reassuring her that all was well.

Soon she started to lay the table for breakfast and load the washing machine before getting side-tracked by pre-Christmas preparations. As she did so she turned on the local radio hoping to hear some of her favourite carols being played; they always brought back some wonderful memories. On the hour, however, the news bulletin caught her attention when it announced that a dangerous prisoner had escaped from Barton, the nearby prison, and she felt a cold shiver run the length of her spine. Turning her gaze towards the front window, she noticed that there were already police gathering in the vicinity and there seemed to be considerable activity.

Suddenly there was a thunderous knock on her front door, causing her to freeze momentarily. It was at times like these that she really missed her husband, Jack; he always reassured her and would have known what to do. At the second pounding she moved into the hall and found herself slipping the chain across the door before cautiously releasing the latch.

"Sorry to disturb you, Mrs Reid, but could we have a word? I am Detective Sergeant Birkett and this is my partner, Sergeant Cooper."

The two men stood assertively in the porch displaying their respective IDs. Marion was caught off balance and staggered awkwardly as she undid the chain and let them in.

Once inside, the officers held out a photo of the man they were looking for – the escaped prisoner – and asked her if she had seen this man and whether there were other people in the house. She explained that her family were here and were all still asleep in bed, but this did not satisfy their curiosity; they wanted to take a look in all the rooms and check out the identities of the people upstairs.

"This is just a formality, Mrs Reid, and to ensure your own safety. No need to be alarmed," DS Birkett reassured her.

She realised that she probably looked rather anxious following the request to see everyone but what was really worrying her was the likeness of the photo to her younger son, Mark.

The officers wasted no time sticking their heads into the dining room and lounge, checking behind the long curtains which she hadn't yet drawn back. They seemed oblivious to the Christmas tree, which had been carefully decorated the day before, and brushed against it carelessly, much to her annoyance.

Nervously, she followed them up the stairs to the bedrooms. They allowed her to enter first to alert the sleeping figures and then DS Birkett asked them to show their faces. Bewildered, Lorna and Gus peered out from the covers feeling awkwardly exposed. The air had chilled as the men swept into the room. Marion could see that Lorna felt quite vulnerable, trapped in this surreal moment. No, it wasn't a dream; they were all part of this unlikely scenario.

Jamie and Mark were still sound asleep next door, snoring in fact! Marion wasn't sure what state the room would be in since they had stumbled into bed, late last night. The fact that the room was dishevelled was the least of her worries though, since she was still concerned about Mark's likeness to the photo. Being woken like this did neither of the boys any favours; their scrunched-up faces and bleary, slit eyes rendered them almost unrecognisable, even to their mother. So, the officers dismissed them fairly quickly from their enquiries.

"You have another daughter, you say, Mrs Reid?" Sgt Cooper remarked.

"Yes, she's in the attic."

"We'd better check her out too – just to make sure she's alone up there."

Marion didn't like the implication, but let it pass. They all squeezed up the narrow staircase to find Lisa sitting up provocatively in bed, hair groomed and eyes out on stalks, almost beckoning the men to question her. She'd heard the movements downstairs and had prepared herself for, what she considered, this 'little adventure'! DS Birkett didn't give her the satisfaction of an interview and said no more than, 'Good morning, Miss,' as they ticked her off their list.

As the officers left, they thanked Marion for her time and warned her to be vigilant since the man in question was still likely to be in the neighbourhood. Marion's peaceful moment had dissolved away, consumed by the unsettled start to the day. Although the boys buried themselves under their duvets again, Lisa was already up and on the phone to her friends and Lorna was slowly heading towards the shower room.

So, Marion retreated again to the kitchen, which was the warm spacious hub of the house, and put the kettle on. She knew there would be much to mull over during breakfast. It was no longer dark outside, so she went to raise the blind on the side window to allow a little more light into the room. It shot up more quickly than she expected, and, in a flash, everything changed; the startled face confronting her through the window was just like Mark's, but it was viciously contorted and stared back at her, menacingly.

Hurtling Terror

Richard Hounsfield

Caged alone, the noise was deafening, his vision blurred, sweat pouring from every pore, trying to quell his churning stomach, head raging with stress fed by his mind full of blind terror: HOW THE HELL COULD THIS BE HAPPENING AGAIN?

Indelible flashes of horror punched their way through Roger's attempts at Thinking Clearly Under Pressure: "T-CUP! T-CUP! T-CUP!" he kept shouting at himself, his voice drowned in the cacophony of this buzzing electrical cupboard in the belly of a jetliner, hurtling through the cold black sky at over six hundred miles an hour away from America and now descending menacingly, somewhere south of Iceland towards the UK.

He was squinting – *is that the circuit breaker?* The blood-spattered face of the petrified flight attendant flashed into his mind signifying the moment he knew the cockpit was lost. Now kneeling hard on the floor, oblivious to the pain of sharp rivets indenting his skin, he searched the vibrating blurry electrical panel that he was figuring out while panting a desperate prayer. A massive turbofan jet engine was screaming just nine feet the other side of the metal skin.

"WHICH FUCKING SWITCH IS IT?" Roger yelled at no-one while frantically scanning the dozens of circuit breakers in row after row after row. "AND WHY ME?!" he bawled with foaming adrenalin spraying the words out of his mouth.

Only ten minutes earlier, he was simply minding his

own business at the rear of the aircraft when he suddenly sensed the shockwave of gasps, shouts and screams tearing back through the cabin led by Monica running like you never see in jetliners.

Despite the paralysing fear, Monica's training had kicked in.

"They're both dead, it's a seven-five hundred!" she blurted at Roger, a Flight Engineer friend just going home to see his mum. Code 7500 was the international code for 'Hijack'.

"They're flying this! The transponder's switched off!"

Monica's panic pierced Roger's bewildered stare and he abruptly grasped the enormity of the emergency. Jolted into action, he scanned the floor, lifted the access hatch and dropped through to the Cargo Deck, then dropped again to the Systems Deck containing the nightmare miles of convoluted cables, wiring, plumbing, hydraulics, hatches, cupboards and fastenings.

"OH SWEET LORD HELP ME NOW." And then he spotted the circuit breaker, conspicuously upright compared with the others face down. This was the moment.

Nobody knew he was here but soon everybody would know he was here. The hijackers didn't know an engineer had been standing aft by an access hatch when they launched their murderous attack; the aircrew didn't know but dead or alive that didn't matter anymore; and it was best the passengers didn't know their fate was being decided in the next ten seconds by him being here.

Roger had to get a grip. The dripping sweat was stinging his eyes and his hands were slippery on the shaking electric panel grab handles. Nobody in the aviation world ever wants to be another Malaysia Airlines 370 vanishing from the earth, all souls missing. That just cannot happen again. The hijackers had switched off the transmitter-responder, the transponder that beams the plane's location onto the air traffic control screens, thus effectively cloaking the plane and disguising its direction. It *must* go back on.

Heart-wrenchingly, Roger knew the terrifyingly inescapable and crushing truth that restarting the transponder would alert the scrambled RAF Typhoon jet fighters racing at twice the speed of sound, frantically scanning and searching to laser-focus their reluctant doom on this hurtling human-filled bomb.

The destiny of three hundred and thirteen would be fated by Roger's next move. He could either collapse sobbing and unleash the shrieking violence of four hundred tons of steel, suitcases and tortured souls at devastating velocity on some innocent UK target unwittingly waiting below; or, should he flick the switch and light up the plane with a beacon that loudly announces 'Here we are!' while also pathetically whimpering... 'A sitting target dying alone to save the living,' before an air-to-air missile tears in to detonate with explosive carnage?

Roger thought of his mum; he knew what was right, but his head was pounding, his eyeballs pulsating and his brain frying with the insane intensity of voluntary death; buffeted by the howling agony of the screaming aircraft and the surging jets, he stretched out his hand with trembling fingers straining for the switch...

But the fateful decision wasn't Roger's to take. In a crowded Whitehall COBRA bunker stood a brand new, dishevelled, blond-haired Prime Minister, eyes transfixed on the intel screens, fidgeting nervously and scared stiff by the rocketing realisation that his much-coveted job was so much more than just 'getting Brexit done'.

The Arrest

Lorraine Surridge

There are two things I like to think I do well and they are baking bread and being a good judge of character. So it was a complete surprise this morning whilst baking my second batch of soda bread at 4.30 a.m. that I watched in disbelief out of my kitchen window as my lovely neighbour Pauline was taken away by police. I wouldn't normally have been so alarmed. Here by the coast it's not unusual for police to collect a relative and drive them to a hospital after a sea rescue or boating accident. However, it would be unusual for them to be made to wear handcuffs.

Absentmindedly I set my timer for the soda bread and checked on my other artisan bakes. The first batch of soda bread along with some ciabatta had already been sorted and I just needed to add the now cooling walnut and raisin loaves to the remaining orders. Young Kenny would be here in fifty minutes to collect and start delivering to the dozen boutique B&B customers I had accumulated in recent months.

Preparing the day's bread for my customers would normally have had my full attention but I just couldn't get the sight of Pauline being taken away out of my mind, and then it hit me. Pauline had still been wearing her pyjamas. She would need a change of clothes at the police station, wouldn't she?

As I checked the time left for the bread, I realised that I would have a window of a few minutes to pick up some clothes for her by nipping next door and letting myself in with the spare key I held for emergencies. Later this morning I could telephone the local police station and see if they could tell me where Pauline was and ask if I could drop off the clothes at some point after I had sold all my remaining soda bread.

Stepping briskly out of my low stable door I went over to Pauline's and let myself in through her kitchen door. Walking purposefully through her blue and white galley-style kitchen, aware that I had just a few minutes to complete the task, I ascended her steep carpeted staircase to the first floor of her cottage.

Pauline had three rooms upstairs, two of which were bedrooms and the other a family bathroom. Just as I went to open what I thought to be the master bedroom door I remembered her saying that she kept her clothes in a walk-in wardrobe in the back bedroom. Upon opening this door, I found it was very dark inside, so I felt along the wall for a light switch. Turning on the light in the back bedroom I was frankly startled to be confronted by a highly decorated room in shades of yellow, pink and green all illuminated by an antique glass chandelier. There was a blackout blind closed over the window with a vivid hummingbird design covering the whole surface. The doors to what I thought must be the walk-in wardrobe were to the right of the window. As I touched the handle, I realised the door was covered in a brushed velvet material. All very opulent, I thought, and wondered, rather uncharitably, as a pensioner how she could afford it.

Pulling the handle on one side the wardrobe door slid across in a concertina style. Slipping in through the gap my head skimmed a string hanging from the ceiling which I thought must be a light pull but when I pulled it nothing happened. The light from the chandelier in the bedroom allowed me to see well enough and I quickly collected some slacks, and a cotton blouse. Then I started to open some drawers looking for underwear. The reduced light was making it more difficult to see inside the drawers, so I knelt closer to search. It was then that I spotted a sliver of light at floor level coming from the back of the wardrobe. Curiosity got the better of me and I felt the wall where the light was coming from, assuming it would be a reflection on something shiny at the back of the wardrobe wall. I nearly fainted when the wall swung open to reveal an inner room.

I couldn't believe my eyes. I stood there open-mouthed probably for only a few seconds, but which seemed like a lifetime. What I saw sent me running out of the house still holding the top and trousers. Returning home, I removed the bread from the oven, set it aside to cool and finished the bread orders in a daze just as Kenny knocked on the door.

"All ready for me, Mrs B?" Kenny asked.

In silence I pointed at the table.

"Everything all right?" Kenny asked in a concerned voice. It was then I blurted it all out and now Kenny, too, stood there open-mouthed.

During the next four hours local people came and went buying the freshly baked soda bread from my kitchen door. To each one in turn, I shared what I had seen until I had sold out of bread. Word spread. People dropped by asking me if what they had heard was true.

So it was with utter astonishment that a little after midday I watched a taxi drop Pauline off at her cottage. Seeing me she waved light-heartedly and walked up to my door. I stepped aside in silence to let her in as she gabbled on excitedly.

"Well, that's one off my bucket list," she concluded.

"I'm sorry Pauline, I don't understand," I gabbled.

"It's my birthday and my son in Australia arranged for an old school friend of his who's now in the police to pretend to arrest me. You know, all those things you want to experience before you go, well my son thought that getting arrested would be one on my list. It isn't actually, but it was kind of him to arrange it."

I looked at Pauline and she could see I was not following her. It was then that she caught sight of the blouse.

"Oh, you've got a blouse like mine," she said.

"It is yours," I whispered. "So, you weren't arrested for what is in that room?" I asked pointlessly.

When people say that a person's face changed as the mask dropped you don't really appreciate what they mean until you see it happen.

Lovely neighbour Pauline had instantly become angry, vicious Pauline. She lashed out at me just as we both heard the approaching sirens.

"You interfering bitch," she snarled as she raced out of my kitchen door and away down the lane.

Sadly, I had to admit to myself that I was not the good judge of character I thought I was. If I had been, perhaps it would have occurred to me that she would have a fake passport and cash stashed in a nearby lockup garage all funded by the proceeds from the hidden cannabis factory behind her walk-in wardrobe.

The Kitchen

Emma Barratt

The terrifying question haunting me was whether to ask Josie or not. It was 4 a.m. and I was awake, staring at our flat white ceiling. A thundering shudder from the digital Samsung washing machine in a perfect towel spin had woken me. The early hours are often when I like to do my thinking; I can then shift problems away like declining calls on a mobile. I can hold the dark storm and shape it to my own ends.

It was raining hard outside and the rhythmic sound of the water running over a blocked gutter, crashing onto the old metal bins beneath, matched my heartbeat. My greying husband, wheezing and snoring loud enough to wake the dead, was in a deep sleep. I was so angry and I wanted to hate him for it. I lifted the feather duvet and slid out, wrapped my silk dressing gown around me and crept down the wide, carpeted main staircase. The fire was still alight in the drawing room, so I sat down and let the velvet-covered armchair envelop me. I reached over and threw another oak log on the dwindling fire and watched the orange flare as it caught. I took deep breaths as Dr June had recommended; in for seven seconds, out for eight. It made my fingers tingle, and I could feel my lungs start to heave. I firmly stuck my perfectly manicured nails into the palms of my soft hands. The pain surged through me. I felt like the dark storm was burying me. I knew I needed to think logically and lucidly to get through this.

My older sister Josie's hatred of me was habitual,

callous and born of enforced shared captivity. On the necessary occasions when we still ended up in each other's company, our curt conversations would be peppered with vitriol and disdain. Josie would use her hefty height to intimidate me. She would push herself into my personal space, often making me back up against the nearest wall. She would smile and took pleasure in frightening me. Now it was an awful truth that I might need to manipulate her to my own ends, to trust and rely on her. The realisation that my daughter's life may depend on Josie's compliance made me lightheaded and nauseous.

I got up and went into the dimly lit kitchen and opened the cupboard under the sink, grabbed the torch and used it to find the hidden key for the cellar. After opening the unwieldy cellar door, I swept the torch from side to side, checking for spiralling spiders. I detested them. The stone steps felt cold and damp beneath my bare feet as I descended into the empty cellar, we never seemed to live long enough in one place to hoard our belongings. Everything in our house was functional. I knew exactly where the correct brick was. I ran my fingers around it and located the concealed button. The brick slid out smoothly and revealed a space behind it. It had taken the engineer two hours to create this secret space and he had willingly accepted cash and agreed to be discreet. I used the torch to check for more angry arachnids, but all that sat there, glinting in the torch beam, was my small brass box. I wriggled out the box, scraping my fingers a little and placed it carefully in my dressing gown pocket. I quickly returned the brick to its former place, brushing the wall a little to disguise the disturbance.

My senses were alarmed by something so I held my breath, stood ram-rod still and listened for the slightest sound. I gradually relaxed as I realised all I could hear was the distant rain and rumbling washing machine. I returned to the hallway which felt warm and surprisingly comforting as I stood listening for my husband's deep-sleep snoring. In the drawing room, I placed another log on the fire and sat again. I clutched the ends of the arms of the chair; I held on so tightly. One by one I made myself release my fingers. I stretched my feet towards the fire seeking that prickling warmth to chase away my fear. Retrieving the box from my pocket I gazed at the intricate carvings and inlaid pearl, easily identifying my secret Celtic name carefully hidden in the design.

I opened the box and retrieved the USB drive. I never thought that I would have to hand on all it contained while I was still alive. I thought I was protected until the next world invited me in.

Josie would demand a payment before agreeing to anything I asked of her. As we had travelled from one continent to another, I had occasionally purchased investment jewellery pieces with cash payments made to me for services rendered. I had never imagined that an early curiosity in online security systems would become such a lucrative, if secret, career. Carrying cash across borders was always difficult, but when I wore my earnings, agencies were less vigilant. I estimated that I had amassed a fund of nearly five million pounds, enough to keep my daughter safe until she reached adulthood. I looked up at her smiling, graceful picture on the mantelpiece. I would prefer her to always remain happily oblivious but that was naïve and probably dangerous. She would need to protect herself one day.

Would Josie give up all she had ever known to save the life of the daughter of her nemesis? Josie was never going to understand why I needed to leave, abandoning all that I loved. I knew she would never forgive me for the past, to protect a future from which she would not directly benefit. I had to find another way forward. The warning had been clear.

I went to the kitchen and retrieved my laptop. I plugged in the USB drive and entered the ancient password, AMBASMESTAS. The word and meaning were engraved in my memory. Confluence, the meeting of rivers and of pathways, a mapped out journey I had to take. An inherited existence passed from mother to eldest child for generations. There was so much to protect.

I clicked, scrolled and searched through the ancient documents looking for an answer, a way out, a clue to a safe place to hide. I read until the light began to seep under the drawn curtains and the fire had gone cold. My limbs had stiffened and the lack of sleep was catching up with me. I had only a glimpse of salvation. I gently removed the USB drive from my laptop, returned it to its box and took it back to its hiding place in the cellar. I locked the cellar door behind me, returned the key to its hiding place and climbed the stairs, desperate for the warm pummelling of our power shower that would hopefully warm and soothe my tired mind. I winced as Alexa's 7 a.m. alarm blasted Wagner into the bedroom over the Bose sound system. The fresh mint toothpaste hurt my teeth, my floral perfume filled my nostrils and stung. My husband rose without saying a word to me and left the room. I paused after dressing and looked out over our neat, ordered garden, the straight beds, edged with stone and filled with white roses, French lavender and lily of the valley. Nothing was out of place, the security cameras swung round slowly taking it all in, the high wall, the spiked metal gates. As I turned to leave, I caught my reflection in the Georgian mirror. I disliked my neat, tailored trousers and cream high-necked shirt. I sighed and turned to finish taming my auburn curls into a tight round bun. One thing I was certain about, I was determined my secret would be protected.

As I sat at breakfast, I heard the thump of post on the bristle door mat. The usual bills and bank statements were flicked through but then my husband handed me a long cream envelope addressed in a beautiful curling script that I did not recognise. I looked up at him but he was not remotely interested in me. I withdrew the bonded card invitation from the envelope, a party, a time, an address but no signatory. I checked the envelope and turned it over for a return address. I even lifted the envelope to my nose hunting for a trace of any clue. Its weight and feel revealed only that it was expensive.

I looked round me, the cold marble surfaces, the glass-top table, the thick navy curtains discreetly distracting the eye from the bars across the windows. I shivered.

I decided I would go to the party, for I was not the only invitee, my daughter's name was typed by mine. I felt a flush rise to my cheeks. I glanced again at my husband and realised he was still oblivious. He was calm, silent and focussed as he finished his breakfast, checked that final email, returned upstairs to dress and completed his final preparations to take our daughter to her private girls' school. My daughter had been sitting to one side reading, or so I thought. Yet when I turned to look for her, I realised that she had been watching me, taking it all in. I smiled.

"An invitation, darling, isn't that marvellous, don't you think?"

She nodded.

"I think we should go. It's on Friday afternoon at five. That will give us time to change after school. It's a tea party for Laila." I had lied.

"OK, Mum, I would like to go."

I watched as she finished brushing her hair, bent to tie the laces on her regulation brown school shoes, did the bronze buttons up on her blazer and adjusted the round, ribbon-trimmed, felt hat. The stern brown uniform did not really flatter her colouring, so like my own.

Suddenly she walked towards me, threw her arms around my waist, leant in close and held on as if her life depended on it. I stroked her soft, dark hair gently before wrapping my arms around her and using all my senses to drink her in. All I wanted was to hold her close, keep her away from any sort of threat.

As her father called from the hallway she let go.

"Goodbye, Mum, see you later... at four?"

"Of course, darling, I will be there."

"Bye, I love you."

"I love you too, darling."

She turned and picked up her school satchel. There was a moment's hesitation, as if she was making a decision, before she walked out of the room. It struck me that she seemed aware that something was amiss. She was painfully observant, and her intuition was always acute. Since turning 11 she seemed to be contained by a new wisdom.

I cleaned up the breakfast detritus slowly, my tired limbs and mind stalling. I was going to have to take my daughter and find somewhere to hide. In the days of constant surveillance we now live in, my every move was going to need careful planning. Tiredness pursued me; all I really wanted to do was sleep. As I stood in the quiet kitchen holding my warm cup of coffee in my cold hands, I noticed a pattern spiralling across the floor. The sunlight, ignoring the bars on the window was decorating my black shoes. I stared, mesmerised. I knew then, in that moment we were escaping together, I would not leave my daughter behind. The decision was made and I would need to plan, meticulously. I picked up the invitation and smiled.

The Doorbell

Lorraine Surridge

So let me tell you how it all started three years ago. Oh God, not again.

It had not taken long for a pleasant *ding dong* to become a mental torture. A type of anonymous mind game.

Every night for two months the doorbell had rung at 1.30 a.m. At first it was annoying. Someone was deliberately disturbing my sleep by ringing my doorbell and disappearing before I could answer the door. It had started on a Saturday and at first, I put it down to louts using the landing along the block of flats to get home. It happened on Sunday as well, and I was further baffled when it continued through the week. The week became a month and now two months had elapsed.

As an ex-soldier would, I reviewed the situation, planned my campaign, and deployed my tactics.

I ignored it; I ran to the door when it rang; I sat near the door; I left the door ajar; I installed a spy hole and sat underneath it; I installed a bell push camera that could be viewed from my mobile phone. Still it rang, and still, nobody was there when I looked out.

I am ashamed to admit that I became vindictive too. I dowsed the bell in all manner of vile substances including superglue but somehow the bell still rang.

Never one normally to give in, I finally came to the decision to remove the bell altogether. That night I got ready to enjoy the first full night's sleep I had had for more than 60 nights. Indeed, I felt so relieved to have removed that cursed bell that I was out like a light as soon as my head hit the pillow.

Oh God, no! Surely not!

I awoke instantly at the sound. Rebuking myself, I shouted out, "It can't be, you stupid fool, it's no longer there!"

I went back to sleep. Well, I say sleep, I just lay there with my eyes closed hoping sleep would come. I rose at daylight and after filling the kettle for a morning cuppa I could not resist the temptation to check any longer. Surely the doorbell could not have rung, I had dismantled it.

Surprised at how much courage it needed, I pulled my shoulders back, took a deep breath and opened the door.

"Gone, thank God!" I shouted rather louder than I meant to. Two teenagers sniggered as they looked back along the landing at me.

"Stupid old git!" one said to the other.

Perhaps they were right. Had senility set in?

As I stared into my now cold cup of tea I vaguely picked up on an interview on the radio. The speaker was talking about their lifelong struggle from trauma. An ex-soldier perhaps. Now I was interested and listened carefully but to my annoyance I had missed most of the interview and the presenter was moving on to another story. No, it wasn't another story, it was a follow-up story with a doctor explaining the hidden illnesses caused by post-traumatic stress disorder.

Well, blow me down. I whistled through my teeth. The words the doctor said resounded in my head:

"Yes, it could be triggered years later by something

unexpected, a smell, a word, a sound as simple as say a door closing or perhaps the ringing of a bell."

Then the shaking and the sweats came. I sat, unable to move, drenched from head to toe. The radio programme had long since ended but still I sat rooted to the spot. Who would have thought that all these years later I would be taken back to that time and that awful place?

It took ten weeks to get an appointment with the psychiatrist. It took another ten weeks for the doorbell to stop 'ringing' at 1.30 a.m. It probably had been louts playing a trick on that first Saturday morning. That small, inconsiderate prank had triggered the deeply buried mental anguish we had endured as hostages waiting for the bell to ring when one by one we would be removed to face our fate. I was told that the bell was a figment of my imagination. It represented memories I had buried and not dealt with. True, I had never spoken to anyone about that time, we just didn't in our day.

I concluded, "This is why I am here speaking to you today. There is no shame in admitting your mental health has been compromised. By chance I survived when our captors fled, expecting a raid was imminent. But I hadn't escaped the mental trauma it had inflicted upon me. If there is just one thing I would like you to take away with you today it's that it's never too late to get help. Installing my new doorbell was a step to freedom in so many ways."

The Besuited Man

Garry Giles

I had started catching the 07:54 bus into town so that I could stop for a cup of tea and then get the shopping that I needed. The 7:54 was usually a fairly fun bus to catch for as well as us older people at the bus stop, there were three other regular passengers who also joined the throng of people already on the bus. A lad who looked around 15, and given that he wore school uniform, I assumed that he hadn't made sixth form yet. He was usually having a sneaky fag as he walked along the road. Then there were two girls who got on the bus too. The older one was obviously a sixth former as the younger girl was in uniform. Whenever I see them it makes me think of the film *The Railway Children*. The older girl was elegant in the same way as Jenny Agutter; the younger one, a bit cheeky like Sally Thompsett. The boy walking along the road completes the trio.

On this particular day though there was also a besuited man on the bus. He looked very out of place and also very alone and was busy reading something. I wondered where his journey started from, given that this bus starts in a rural village. Where could he be going?

I enjoy shopping earlier in the morning: the displays at the fish counter are so spectacular, and I am sure that I will meet the other shoppers that I know. We go out before the school-run shoppers, and we know that there will be space; time to shop; and, just as importantly, time for a chat.

Once in town on this particular day I was inevitably meeting and greeting the people that I know to a greater or lesser degree. I stopped for my cup of tea before gathering the bits of shopping that I needed. I had plenty of time before the bus took me back home. I reminded myself to get pencil sharpeners.

I pondered at the shops, the cakes in the bakery window that made me fancy a Chelsea bun, the butcher's shop gave me ideas for tea. Eventually I gathered all that I had gone out for.

While I was waiting for the bus that would return me to home, I wondered about the man on the bus. My mind drifted to a Paul Simon song where he describes being on a Greyhound bus with his girlfriend, comparing people's faces and imagining that one of them was a spy. But why would a spy be here on a country bus? Surely I am just fantasising now.

Back at home I was busy working but I couldn't get the strangeness of the 'out of place' appearance of this man out of my mind. Almost obsessively I printed out the bus timetable and watched each one of the buses go by to see if he was on it. One after the other passed by, then finally I saw him on the 17:43. I thought surely, he must be going out to one of the villages. Knowing this just made the puzzle even more curious. Although I didn't need any more shopping I decided to be on that bus!

The next morning, I was at the bus stop with five others (including the three schoolkids) and along came the 7:54. He was there and so I sat next to him. He was reading something on an iPad.

"Good morning," I said.

"And good morning to you," was the reply.

I asked him where he was off to.

"Oh, I'm riding on a couple of buses and working remotely somewhere," was the enigmatic response.

"Where will that be?"

"I haven't decided yet. It's an experiment, you see. I bid you good day."

And he was off!

An experiment? What kind of experiment was he undertaking? I was on the verge of following him as it was going to take ages to find out anything on these short journeys into town. But part of me thought that I shouldn't as it would be so obviously nosey. Was I becoming a stalker?

Then I noticed him getting onto a double-decker bus and going upstairs, so, with inquisitiveness getting the better of me, I joined the queue and sat downstairs so that I could see where he got off. It wasn't until the end of the route that he came down the stairs. *What do I do now?* I thought.

I realised that he had disappeared and I found myself to be somewhere that I did not intend to be, nor particularly wanted to be. *Oh well,* I thought, *I may as well have a cup of tea in the terminus café.* The people in the café who are waiting for the bus seem to be loaded with bags. They had been to the shopping centre, and I found that I was fascinated by how much they were carrying. They clearly had a purpose whereas I just followed a whim.

While I was thinking about what to do, I was surprised to see the man reappear and board the bus for the return journey. I decided to join him and try to engage with him again. It was a single-decker bus so I sat in the double seat in front of him.

"Hello again," I said.

"Well good day; you must be a bus traveller like me."

"I do enjoy getting around; and apologies if I'm being intrusive but you are always reading on your iPad: are you a bit of a bookworm?"

"Actually, I'm reading legal papers that I usually do on the number 88 bus in London, although this is an experiment to see whether I view things differently in the countryside."

I left him alone to his work and sat wondering for the half-an-hour return journey.

On arriving home, I looked up the number 88 bus route and then the realisation came. He was 'the man on the Clapham Omnibus'!

Amir

Joyce Smith

The banging infiltrated his brain in the guise of a dream but coalesced into reality when he realised someone was assaulting his door in the early hours of the morning. He heard his neighbour shouting, "They're coming, Amir."

Already dressed, having fallen exhausted onto his bed without undressing the night before. Amir grabbed his bag and made for the window. Lowering himself down, he escaped through the olive trees into the shadows of the hills behind his house.

His bag was packed not only with his medical equipment but a few items for survival prepared for this very situation. As a Jew, he knew his presence in Iraq was governed by his profession and how useful his services were to the local authorities. Having been posted to western Iraq, a poor desert area, he was soon caught up in a smallpox outbreak and had set up a quarantine house. Since then he had been left alone to follow his profession. Since the *coup d'état* in 1941, by Arab Nationalists, sympathetic to the Nazi regime in Germany, his existence had become more precarious. With the attack on his door, he knew the situation had taken a dangerous turn.

He made his way up into the brown earth hills past the occasional stunted olive tree and scrub-defined shapes of old dried-up rivers. Avoiding the patches of moonlight, hiding as best as he could amongst the bushes, he hunkered down to wait. The night seemed interminable and his intermittent and uneasy sleep was disturbed a couple of times by the snuffling of wild boar as they rooted around. This situation had happened before, and he knew his seekers would carry on to another village when they found him gone. For the most part, he lived in an uneasy peace with his Muslim neighbours. They valued his presence as a doctor. Now and again, however, a group of Sunni hotheads would try to seek him out. The following night he made his way down to find his home ransacked, furniture and household items broken and patients desperate for his help. This was blatant and violent, and he wondered what would have happened to him if they had caught up with him. He was heartbroken at the destruction and what it meant.

A few days later, he packed up his few belongings and made his way out of the village. The epidemic was nearing its end and his patients were no longer infectious. He trekked for many days with just his donkey for company until he reached the city of Ramadi. Tired and dusty, he went straight to the Jewish quarter where he had relations. He was greeted with much pleasure and joy as they had not seen him for many years. Life was easier in the cities because there was usually a sizeable Jewish community, respected and welcomed for their expertise in the fields of finance and commerce. His uncle was a banker and Amir thought he might be able to help.

Amir's uncle had always liked Amir and was persuaded by his wife to help the young man. Amir was duly installed in his own practice within the boundaries of the city. After a slow start the practice prospered and even Muslims came to seek his advice. He gained a reputation as a good and hardworking doctor. He began to relax and when the idea of a wife was put to him by the local marriage broker, he acquiesced and was introduced to the beautiful Sara. They married and they were blessed with a son and then a daughter. This new-found peace, however, was not to last. The influx of Jews in the middle east from Nazi Germany and the rise of Zionism upset the Arabs in the city and the setting up of the state of Israel was the last straw for many. Anti-Jewish slogans were painted on the outside of the practice. Amir's children were bullied and picked on in school. One night a group of Muslim youths gathered outside Amir's home, shouting and throwing stones. The police were called but did little to stop the abuse. Once again, Amir had to make the difficult choice to leave, this time taking his wife and children.

The morning of their departure, Amir was disturbed to find a delegation of local Muslim dignitaries, outside his door, headed up by the local Mujahidin. Fearful of why they had come, he bravely opened the door and faced them. He welcomed them into his home and waited to hear what they had to say. After much shuffling of feet and clearing of throats, the Mujahidin apologised for the behaviour of the young Arab men and in a long-winded and roundabout way, praised Amir's work in the community and eventually asked him to stay. He was promised that there would be no more trouble.

That evening, sitting up on their roof terrace surrounded by date palms, oleanders and hibiscus scenting the air, Amir and his family sat looking at the sunset. He knew, for now, that Ramadi was their home.

1.30 a.m.

Sarah-Jane Reeve

Was that the doorbell? I wake up and grab my phone from the bedside table. It's 1.30 a.m. I've only been asleep an hour and a half. Is it one of the girls? They've forgotten their key. I lay awake and listen. No one calls. No plaintive cries of, "Mum!" What am I thinking? They're both at uni.

My husband beside me turns over and sleepily mutters some protest about a meeting in the morning. The noise was probably kids in the street messing about. Then silence. Slowly I pull up the duvet, and sink down into black sleepy depths.

There it is again! That was definitely the doorbell. I switch on the phone again. 3 a.m.! Oh, this is no joke. Adrenalin flows. I grab my robe and get up. Maybe it's the next-door neighbours; perhaps it's an emergency. I should really check. But I don't know who is out there. Fearing burglary on the doorstep, I go downstairs to the front door, flick the porch light switch and look through the spyhole. No one. For good measure I go into the sitting room to the window looking out onto the drive. A few leaves blow across the flowerbeds, and I can only see an old fox with a broken tail trotting across the road. Well, my heart is pounding and I'm well and truly awake now. I'll make tea and read.

A few minutes later, I'm settled on the sofa, moving the cat over and grabbing the blanket. The cat looks up in surprise but snuggles up to me, grateful for the shared body heat. I drink my tea, read a page and feel myself drifting. In the distance I can hear the faint noise of the engineering works at the railway station. I turn off the lamp. I'll just sleep here. It's cosy here with the purring cat.

Was that a knock on the door? I check the time by the dining room clock: 5 a.m. Deliveries don't arrive this early. Or do they? I check the spyhole again. By this time the sky is streaked with the grey of dawn. One or two birds tentatively start to twitter. I am cold now and stiff from the sofa. I trudge up the stairs to bed.

Now I can hear footsteps on the ceiling! I slowly realise the local magpies are running up and down the roof over my bedroom like they're running races on sports day. I check the time on my phone. How can it be 8 a.m.? The sunlight is tactlessly forcing its way through the gaps in the curtains. Jane-next-door starts her car and drives off to work. There's whistling from the bathroom as Paul shaves. With a leaden head I groan, and ignore the hypnotic stare of the cat who has just materialised beside me.

"Don't be fooled. I've already fed her," says Paul. "I was awake so I thought I might as well get up and write that report."

Paul does his push-ups and grabs his shirt with the energy of a well-rested man. I mutter incoherently about being up in the night.

"Not 'doorbell dreams' again!" he laughs.

"I'm always convinced they're real," I sigh.

The Woman On The Bus

Joyce Smith

She looked out of place. A beautiful, elegant woman on a London bus. The kind of woman who could wave an imperious hand and, as if by magic, a taxi or even a limousine would appear. She was always on the same bus. The one that took me home after my day's work at the office, the number 9 bus which left King's Cross at precisely 6.15 every evening. Elegantly dressed, she sat up very straight, looking ahead. She always wore gloves and clutched a small matching handbag. Her hair was beautifully coiffed in an elegant French plait. She was an enigma, and I began to wonder about her. Perhaps she was some great lady who had fallen on hard times. Maybe she was going to visit someone and did not want anyone to know. Although the bus was crowded at that time of night, she always sat in the same seat, front row window, behind the driver.

One night, after a particularly exhausting day at work, I fell asleep on the bus. I woke up at the terminal in time to see the woman alight with the aid of the driver's hand. He then escorted her into the ladies' waiting room and hurried off, I presume to clock off after his shift. I wearily made my way over to the bus station cafeteria to buy some refreshment and wait for a bus back. There was only one other person in there and I made my way to the counter. After ordering a coffee and a rather stale-looking bun, the woman serving said she would bring my order to me. I sat down nearby. I was in the middle of drinking my coffee, having abandoned the bun, when I noticed the elegant

48

woman from the bus leaving the terminal. Soon after, the driver came out of the office and left in the same direction. The woman who had served me noticed my interest. By that time, I was her only customer.

"Rum couple, aren't they?" she said.

I looked at her with interest.

"Couple?" I said. "What! They're married?"

"Oh yeah." She leaned towards me. "Sad story. She is the daughter of a lord and he was her chauffeur. They fell in love and ran away together."

I suddenly noticed the time and realised I was going to miss my bus. I made a regretful farewell and ran for my ride home.

As I had a week's holiday owing I decided to take the next week off and play some golf. When I caught the bus after my first day back, the woman was not there. After a week without her presence, I was full of curiosity and decided that I would carry on to the terminal on the bus and see what I could find out. The driver climbed wearily down from the bus and made his way over to the office. I went into the cafeteria, hoping the same woman would be serving. Once again, we were on our own. She came over to my table with my coffee and we carried on, as if there had been no interruption, with our earlier conversation.

"So sad," she said. "He had to have her sectioned in the end. To cut a long story short, they had a child, a little girl. There was a terrible accident. The child drowned. What made it worse, her family refused to come to the funeral. She never got over it. The only way he could keep an eye on her was to have her travel with him. Last week she suddenly got off the bus in the middle of the journey. Fortunately, he saw her leave and chased after her, but realised he could no longer look after her."

I sat for some time over my cooling coffee thinking about the beautiful woman and her sad story and of other people on other buses with their own stories to tell, and I did not even notice when my own bus left.

It was about a week later when I was sitting on the bus again when a large middle-aged woman, overloaded with shopping, came and sat next to me. I moved over and she thanked me profusely.

"That's a lot of shopping. Have you far to go when you get off the bus?" I asked.

"Oh, it's all right, love," she said, "my hubby's the driver. I go as far as the terminal so he can help me take it all home. We always stop and have a bite to eat in the cafeteria with Vera. Not a bad cup of coffee and she's always got a good story to tell, has Vera. I'm sure she makes them up most of the time."

CHAPTER 2

NATURAL WONDERS

Autumn

Joyce Smith

A catalyst between summer's calm
And winter's bitter rage
A magnificent madness
Drama on a dark lit stage

Dervish trees join in the dance
Wind alive, they bend and whip
Birds swoop between their branches
Aware of their span and wing tip

Leaves spiral down, rain wet
A last glorious kaleidoscope
Before they reach the muddy ground
Or swirl sideways, their last hope

Small animals chase and forage
Hiding their hibernal feast
Knowing there will be no more
Until the winter's ceased

We abandon our gardens
To the winter's justice
Count the days to spring
And await nature's promise

Oh Colourful You

Garry Giles

You flit and you fly through my life
Though you are gone in the blink of an eye
So what are you going to do
Oh colourful you?

All I know about you, which seems unjust
Is that you are way down in the food chain
For birds; mammals; and even insects
You are merely their prey

Some superstitious people fear you
A 'Death Omen' they would say
That is if there are three of you
Though others disagree

'To see three white butterflies is lucky'
Is *their* mantra
Maybe you are just misunderstood
As others just do not want you

They say that you 'nibble' their cabbages
And lay your eggs in unwanted places
And then your caterpillar young
Seem to smile in their faces

I wonder what it is that keeps you going
Caught on the breeze and blown away
Please came back and pollinate
On another sunny day

And then the butterfly landed
As dead as dead could be
Motionless
It made me sad to see what I could see

So, I moved to rest you in peace
And you flew off where the wind blew
Thank you for those moments
Oh colourful you.

Snowfall

Moyra Zaman

The night bit hard, solidifying the land.
A claustrophobic cloud camouflaged the sky at dawn
and the grey grip of day seemed set in stone.

Until a timorous flicker, a frozen raindrop, teased the air;
intermittently others followed, slowly dripping their way
to nothingness, and nothing more.

But the spell was broken and soon a fine flurry whirled
in frenzied agitation, buffeted on the East Wind's whim,
circling down as white flour dusting.

A confusion of confetti followed, tossed on high
performing murmurations, then staking claim
on lacey layers of landscape far below.

Thickening puffs of fluff floated fondly down,
now unmistakably proud to identify as snow,
weaving flakes of 'snow on snow' uniquely into blankets.

Marshmallow mounds took shape protectively,
while barren branches preened their heavy hoar
and shrubs submissively shouldered snow's descent.

The ground's canvas, tempered now in virgin white,
exuded its light, and softly breathed its silence,
suspending lives in childish wonder.

Then, a finale of fizzling flakes floundered to a misty veil
hiding the past and welcoming the fresh fall
of footprints on unadulterated snow.

The Butterfly

Joyce Smith

*H*ow *did I get here?* she thought as she stared out of the window. *In this miserable place that smells of stale cabbage and worse. It's not as if I am really old and infirm, like some.* She had resisted the idea, but her son was quite persuasive.

"No more worries, Mum. No housework or gardening. Meals cooked for you," he said.

She knew he was concerned for her welfare, but she also knew he was tired of the journey once a fortnight. Such a long way to come and make sure she was all right. The home was much closer to where he lived. It was the fall, however, that was the deciding factor. Afterwards, she was in a lot of pain and was easily persuaded that a care home was the best option.

It was a grey day in late spring and the weather could not seem to settle. It was not the best of views. She would rather have had a room that looked onto the garden but there were none available at the time. All she could see was a line of garages with the paint peeling off. The worst thing was the boredom. Although physically impaired, her brain was still active. She had books to read but there was only so much reading she could do and anyway it made her eyes ache after a while. There was a common room, but the television was on so loud because of those with impaired hearing, that nobody talked to each other. She was not interested in the bingo nights or, even worse, Keep Fit from a chair. The main reason, however, for her depressed state was the fact that it was her eightieth birthday, and everybody seemed to have forgotten it.

She was beginning to feel rather sorry for herself when the sun suddenly broke through the clouds. It shone onto her window ledge. The ledge was wide, and she had put the potted geranium her son had brought her on his last visit, onto its surface. She was just admiring the plant, when out of nowhere, the butterfly landed. Gently picking its way over the flowers, she was struck by its fragile beauty, the blue iridescence of its wings which unfolded to show a delicate tracery of markings. She no longer saw the garages with their peeling paint. She sat entranced by the scene before her, the piercing blue of the butterfly set off by the riotous red of the flowers. She did not hear the knock on the door and was startled by the carer walking in holding a clutch of cards in one hand and a huge bunch of flowers in the other.

"Come on, Stella!" she said. "You need to put your best frock on and comb your hair, your son and his family are coming to take you out for the day."

The Storm

Emma Barratt

Friday, August 1831

In the dark slate dawn on the harbour wall of Tobermory the heaped baskets awaited their salty shroud. The soft stench of the grey dappled cod glistening in the drizzle invaded my nostrils. On the smooth-hulled fishing boats, the nets laid out on the decks were rinsed by the rain, hemp ropes cracked against the wooden masts and the edges of sails escaped their bonds and flapped viciously against their bindings.

I started as a Gael called out to me, "Come awa, sir, and buy a calder haddock or fine cod. There's a skatie nae twa hours oot o' th'water."

Shaking my head in acknowledgement I pulled my great coat tightly around myself and marched on. A plume of smoke buffeting out of a square chimney and a candlelit window guided me towards the low-slung, slate-roofed customs house. I slipped on the slick stones as I leaned my body in to open the oak door. I nodded at the scrawny ticket officer whose brass buttons flashed in the flickering candlelight.

"Your name, sir?"

I wrote the name Mr Wilder, Michael Thomas slowly in the ship's manifest. Glancing at the delicate and boldly printed curled script on my ticket, a flicker of excitement flashed through me as I read the words '*Maid of Morvern*, Steamship'. I forced the ticket into my overstuffed pocket while being careful not to let my sketchbook fall. A pale woman with a blue plaid shawl wrapped around her red hair and thin shoulders was standing in front of the glowing coal fire. I felt the building sigh with the wind as I observed her. Her wet, brown leather boots steamed a little from the invading heat as she stood still and erect while trying to warm herself. She was carrying a large brown leather satchel like my own; a fellow artist, I surmised. As I looked to her eyes, she turned her back on me, yet I was certain I had spotted a flicker of recognition.

Turning to the customs officer I asked for directions to the departure point of the rowing boat that would take us to meet the steamship. I left before her and hurried towards the stone pier I had been directed to. I could just make out the remains of a few squat, rotting barrels washed up on the far shore, a legacy of the bankrupt kelp trade. I recalled the conversations over dinner the previous night, the unease on the face of the laird as he described the howls and weeping of the croftsmen and their families as they were forced upon the ships that took them from their ancestors' lands. Lands now abandoned to sheep. I was reminded of the stately great *Temeraire* that was ripped apart, the five thousand oaks used in her building made into tables, chairs and wardrobes before being scattered throughout the homes of England.

I could see the oarsman readying the boat. I climbed slowly down the ladder; the rope felt rough against the palm of my hand and my foot scrabbled for the wooden rung. Once safely in the boat I stared out, savouring the drifting sea mist and rain. I sat and then grabbed the side of the gunwale to retain my balance. I breathed deeply to steady myself. It was with some trepidation that I watched the lady with the red hair being assisted down. The continuing rain prompted the gentlemanly offer of one of the oarsmen's own oilskins for her further protection. Her soft Irish tones rang out clearly as she declined. She sat forward from me, her long back a rebuff to my direct, inquiring gaze.

The small boat creaked and shuddered as it made its way to the wide harbour mouth. It stole past the seals, their slumbering bodies blending into the rocks, a few lazily opening a rounded dark eye.

The splashes of the oars were drowned out by the bristling wind. I watched as her red hair fluttered and escaped her shawl. She seemed not in the least perturbed by the chill, rain or increase in the swell of the waves as we left Rub an Righ behind us and rowed north, up the Sound of Mull.

As we left the safety of the lee of the land the light rose further up in the sky and the white crested waves jostled and played with our vulnerable little boat.

I covered my ears in shock as an ear-splitting roar from the great funnel of the *Maid of Morvern* made me turn. I stared at the enormous frolicsome female bearing down upon us, leaving all manners and decency behind her. Her pugnacious, lumbering motion entranced me as her long thin hooter vented and spilled steam to the sky and over the wild sea. She powered down at full speed while churning and walloping the water. As she grew close and the *Morvern*'s crew spotted us, her power propulsion slowed. The sea heaved around her but the lady eventually stopped, rocking proudly in her own turmoil as another long, piercing hoot blasted out, shooting up the funnel with enough force to split a head.

I wondered at our oarsman's skills as they drew alongside. This brilliant steamship was new to this part of the world and her ability to seemingly stop on a sixpence impressed me. A rope flew through the air and was grasped firmly by the muscled hand of one of the oarsmen who heaved and braced his body against the swell. I struggled up the swaying rope ladder and felt strong arms pull me onto the deck of the *Maid of Morvern*. I laughed with the exhilaration. I was silent as I watched her climb up the rope ladder, surer footed than I was. It was perhaps God's grace that neither of us had slipped and fallen into the sea's icy grip. The small rowing boat cast off and I watched it fighting against tide and wave; I shuddered with the realisation of how weak and vulnerable it was. I felt the engines roar into magnificent life again. What delight it would have brought me to actually see the guts of this great ingenious animal that bore us along.

She stood tall beside me, swaying with the ship yet suddenly she lost her balance. Instinctively I gallantly reached out for her, offering my hand. She rebuffed me, turned away and moved towards the varnished wheel house. I watched her before glancing skyward and was delighted to see the towering grey cumulonimbus, the grandeur and beauty of the threatening storm, extending further across the sky. I drew out my sketchbook and attempted to render on paper the impression of my momentary impending fear.

The ship drove alongside the bays of Mull, the flat fields leading down to cliffs and stony beaches. The land was gentle, green and safe. I ignored it all as my pencil flew, filling page after page. I looked up and strained to see the sun in its hiding place behind the clouds. I drew hard lines, soft shadows and twisted the pencil trying to capture the virulence of it all.

Eventually I entered the wheelhouse in search of food. I looked for her the instant I stepped into the room. She was sat, her scarf draped loosely round her shoulders, red hair flowing down her back curling and teasing itself about her woollen coat. She glowed in the gas light and I felt an overwhelming desire to paint her. She seemed to me like a creature the impending storm had created; charged, powerful. Her blue eyes met mine. I was certain I knew her. I wanted to hold her gaze.

The captain of the ship, in buoyant mood, passed between us and gestured his head towards a table laden with mugs of steaming coffee, a plate of fried fish and bread, oaten biscuits and an overfilled jar of Dundee orange marmalade. I acknowledged the suggestion and started to move towards the table. I looked towards her once again but now she was engaged with her own meal, her eyes downcast.

I sat and shrugged off my coat and satchel. I ate slowly, savoured the fish and enjoyed the tartness of the orange marmalade on the bland oaten biscuit. The coffee surged in my veins, lifting any sense of tiredness that endured from my early start.

My journey had lasted many days to get to this point and I felt finally that I was now on the last furlong. I perused the cabin, curious as to who else was venturing out with us to see the mystical sight of Fingal's Cave, and noticed a gaunt-looking clergyman, wrapped entirely in black, staring fixedly at the horizon through a window. He must have joined the ship at Oban and I surmised the clergyman must have been miserable for quite some time. The poor man was nervously plucking at his coat and repeatedly running his finger around the inside of his collar to loosen it. His hair curled out from under his damp shovel hat while water still dripped from the rim and ran down his collar. He seemed afraid and I sympathised but did not wish to approach him; to do so would have led to unnecessary conversation. My own amiability in the past had meant that when confined to small spaces like this, I had often had to sacrifice my own peace of mind to suit the conveniences of another.

She took off her coat and underneath was a floor-length dress in soft green, closely fitted along her arms with the smallest ruffle at the shoulders. At the neck the collar stood straight and proud. Her waist was small but not restrained by any whalebone stiffening. My mother had often complained of such things. Round her neck was a long silver chain with a locket that hung at her waist. The outfit seemed surprisingly light for her journey and was absent of any other adornment or ribbons. The usual cap often worn in such circumstances was also absent. Her fingers were slender and on her right hand her ring finger bore a gold band which was adorned simply with three blue sapphires. I got out my sketch pad and began to draw. I started with her long rich hair.

She glanced my way once but then returned to writing in a small notebook she had retrieved from her satchel. Deep in concentration, she wrote and wrote. I drew feverishly, hoping to finish before she realised what I was doing. I stared, taking in every shadow, every mark. It was a sweet luxury to observe her like that. I wanted to capture her bravery, her aloneness and the warmth hinted at by the way she smiled at her own written endeavours.

A sharp jolt made me stop what I was doing. I looked toward the windows and realised that the earlier drab grey was deepening. I crossed to the windows to see out. My walk was unsteady and my stomach somersaulted as the ship moved more strongly beneath my feet. Rain prickled the glass of the windows. I was alarmed when I realised I could barely see the coast of Mull. The waves were increasing in number and size, the hue of the sea changing from pale to dark with a chaotic embroidery of white lace waves scattering everywhere. I felt a sudden, urgent desire to taste that briny wildness. I saw the boldness of the waves and wanted to hear the endless crash as they tore themselves at the invaded shore.

I grabbed my coat and headed for the door. She was startled by my movements and realising what I was doing also stood and threw on her coat.

"I'm coming with you."

I firmly shook my head.

"No, it's far too dangerous."

"You are going," she replied while tilting her head to one side. "So am I!"

I hesitated and studied her momentarily while considering my next move. I was not given a chance to decide as she pushed past me, opened the door and went out into the heavy rain. I followed her, breathing in sharply at the shock of the rain soaking my face as I remerged on deck.

"How far to Fingal's Cave from here is it?" she called above the whistling wind.

"A mere half hour at most. I need my drawing things; hold the rail, don't let go. I'm Wilder!"

"Aisling," she cried.

I returned with a rope and we fought our way to the foredeck. Our feet slipped and to counter this we leant forward and into each other as the boat rolled.

"The captain says we are mad, he takes no responsibility for us," I said.

"Silent, be silent! This is wondrous. This is God's wish," she replied.

I gripped the rail as the ship dipped and lurched. At one point the great ship shuddered and seemed to brake before surging forward. The gulls were unfettered and unafraid, lost on the wind, soaring out of control, pushed ever higher, then plunging down to skim the waves.

An enormous wave crashed over the side of the boat, sending freezing sea water skidding across the deck, drenching our clothes and boots. I blinked my eyes and licked my lips to assuage the saltiness burdening them. The barbarian wind raised my blood and roared in my ears. I watched her, coat undone and flapping around her, her hair whipped up, twisted and ravaged into a storm of its own.

I began to stagger towards the bow of the boat and she followed. I was not afraid but nevertheless I tied one end of the rope around my waist and indicated to her what I then wanted to do. I felt her glowing warmth under my deft fingers as I fumbled and attempted to tie the rope around her waist. She stared straight into my eyes, but did not smile. I saw the tiny black flecks in her blue eyes just before she blinked and looked away. I moved closer to the front of the bow and began to tie the other end of the rope around the rail. She stepped closer to me and then leant out over the rail, straining to see ahead.

I drew out my sketchbook and pencil from my pocket and attempted to draw as the sea surged beneath us. The sea's surface darkened, turning from dark green to anthracite grey. The waves grew in size, their white tops spun and spiralled away. I wanted to capture the sea's power, a challenge to my existence; only my pencilled impressions might survive. It was a great work in the making.

I felt gentle pulses of nausea as the swell drove us on and then my legs went from under me, dragging her down beside me. We were tethered together, sat against the white railings and watched the magnificent show unfurl above us. It was sublime. I looked up at the sky and thought I saw the sun. I wiped the water from my face and looked again but I was mistaken. My pencil still circled and swirled as I tried desperately to capture that brief impression of a splash of gilded clouds.

We got closer to Fingal's Cave but then the clouds became heavier, the wind stronger. A sinister swell of the sea gathered. We struggled to our feet. The ship plunged up a mountainous wave before surging down into its valley. The sea was a hurricane of brown and black shadow.

We were terrified and the rain soaked us to the skin. In all her greatness the ship shuddered as she entered the eye of the storm. Amidst this tremendous power she was small and alone. This Atlantic could have swallowed us at any moment yet with imperial heart she ploughed on. As we became unsteady and fearful her spirit spurred me on and I continued to draw.

We could barely see Fingal's Cave as we reached it and I realised that there was no hope of going ashore to explore. The ship gradually stopped and then slowly turned. I drew what I could, peering ahead to capture that mystical sight. Mysteriously, amidst this great maelstrom I saw the sun beyond where vision fades, spinning across the surface of the sea.

Suddenly Aisling cried out, an ear-splitting scream of exhilaration from the depths of her soul. The clamour and commotion propelled me into her arms and I held her, laughing, weeping, offering comfort.

The sea suddenly curved and the ferocious wind whirled over us. A final wondrous wave roared over the bow and still tethered together we were swept along the deck of the ship. As we scrabbled for the door of the wheelhouse I glanced back and was confronted by a vision. Glory was indeed before us. The exploding sea echoed Fingal's Cave as the wind lifted the deafening waves, the rain arched and twisted around the halo of the sun.

We collapsed through the door and lay breathless, cold

and shaking upon the wheelhouse floor. We lay on our backs, her hand in mine, as the priest sank to his knees and prayed.

Saturday, July 1832

Last night I heard Mendelsohn's composition, the Hebrides Overture, at a concert and was immediately drawn back to that fateful trip. His music captured what I had seen, a glorious, mystical place of sublime beauty in nature. I resolved the next day to revisit my painting.

I saw her through the crowd in the Royal Academy. Her red hair flowed down her back over a sea blue dress. She stood lightly, intently studying my painting. I saw her smile. I felt such a rush of pride and delight. I wove through the crowd of dark coats, top hats and gruff male voices, yet as I reached my painting, she had gone.

I stared at what I had painted from my memory and my sketches. The ship boldly steamed forward encompassed by that immense sea. The sunlight glowed on the horizon. Fingal's Cave emerged, wild and dark. As I contemplated my work, I could see my painting of nature at its most ferocious being challenged by humanity with its ingenuity. Yet it was also a painting of the beautiful Aisling, at the glorious moment she was most alive to me.

I'm Being Swept Away

Garry Giles

I can't believe that I'm caught up in this storm. As if the rain were not hard enough to deal with, the wind is making it almost impossible for me to cope. I'm trying to find somewhere to hide away, it's all so violent. The sheer effort to keep stable is taking all my concentration, and I can hardly see where I am going. This may be the end of me.

I really need to stop for a few moments to catch my breath but where is safe? I'm struggling to see a suitable place, so I have to stop where I am. I can't carry on. Now I am blown into a puddle. I'm wetter than I've ever been.

I'm so frustrated, I'm carrying on, but I am feeling totally exhausted. Now I think I can see a place that looks a little safer, and there is a fence at the side to protect me from the wind a little. Now I'm on a ledge and I am protected from the gusts of wind, well at least for now anyway. Will this rain ever relent? I must make my way back to safety. How on earth am I going to do that?

No! I'm being swept away again! Now I'm in an enormous bubbling pool. It's all so fierce. I'm swimming with every last ounce of my energy but I can't see a way out of this swirling wash of water.

I can't see what is happening. My vision is blurred. Is something being held out to me? I'm swimming towards it but the surges are taking me away. I'm so tired.

Wow! My last lunge has got me onto a huge piece of wood. I'm hanging on tight! Slowly I am being lifted up out of this watery hell. I think I'm safe. At last!

The man with the piece of wood felt delighted that he had saved the life of the ladybird that had fallen into the water butt.

CHAPTER 3

ODD MOMENTS

The Escape

Kate Stanley

Looking out one summer's eve
I could scarce believe my eyes.
The knot hole in our garden fence
Had doubled in its size.

Creeping over, nonchalant
I crouched and peeped right through.
What a shock! Oh, *quelle horreur*!
This just could not be true.

Right beside the garden pond
Sat Geoff, my grumpy gnome.
His rod dipped in the murky depths,
He looked so right at home.

Well I never, surely not!
Was I hallucinating?
But when I saw his curly beard
There just was no mistaking.

I planned a rescue mission,
I had to get him back!
But when I really, really looked
Something stopped me in my tracks.

A look of quiet contentment
Glazed his cheery features,
Sitting with his garden friends
And other stony creatures.

My grumpy Geoff was smiling now
With dimpled, plump pink cheeks.
I realised with sudden shame
He'd been missing for three weeks.

He needed cheerful company,
I should have noticed sooner
Poor old Geoff developing
A lonely, sad demeanour.

He's gone to find a better place,
My turn to sulk and pout.
But now I have to just accept
My Geoffrey has moved out.

A Look Through The Keyhole

Lisbeth Cameron

I have a very bright cat which somehow controls all the dogs running loose around here. One day my neighbour's dog entered the kitchen and the cat which was lying on a stool inside the door just hooked one claw into his nose and he ran screaming out.

The other day as I passed the kitchen door, I noticed the cat on top of the table. I have never allowed or seen the cat on the table before. I stopped and peeped into the room. The dining table had just been laid for afternoon tea with sandwiches, tea, sugar, and cream. I realised that there seemed to be a bit of teamwork going on: our dog was waiting beside the table and looked like it was very aware of what was happening. The cat was now pushing the cream jug carefully along the table, with its paw. The dog looked very excited. At the edge of the table the cat very professionally put a paw into the handle and the dog took the jug into his mouth. The cream jug was transported safely down onto the floor.

The cat now jumped down and tipped the jug onto the floor. They both then licked the cream to their heart's delight. The jug was not broken, and I have never seen such teamwork. From beginning to end they looked like partners in crime, and I wondered how many times they had done this trick before.

Vanilla or Chocolate?

Joyce Smith

She was on her way to the clothing section in the supermarket to buy some knickers, when Sue thought she heard someone call her name. She stopped mid stride to listen.

"Sue."

And then she heard, more purposefully, "*Sue.*"

She stopped and looked around, saw no one she knew but caught the wave of someone's hand out of the corner of her eye. She turned to see a woman with hair an unlikely shade of red. Sue stared at her as she hurried over to her.

"Don't you know me? We were at school together. It's Jane," she said as Sue struggled to place her. "We were in the same year at St Margaret's."

When she did recognise Jane, Sue was shocked at the change in her. Gone was the round smiling face with the dimples and the beautiful long fair hair. Jane looked careworn, very thin and her dyed hair was scraped back in a ponytail. Above all, Jane looked frightened. She took Sue's arm and pulled her into an empty aisle.

"I need your help," she said, looking intently into Sue's face. "I can't explain, but I am in danger. My husband," she faltered, "I think he wants to kill me."

Sue stared at her, not believing her ears.

"He is waiting outside in the carpark. I need to get past him. Can you meet me in the toilets? Please," she said when she saw the doubt on Sue's face.

Sue followed her into the ladies' toilets.

"I know it's a lot to ask," Jane begged. "But can we swap coats?"

She looked so scared, Sue felt she had to comply.

"I need you to leave here and go into another shop a few doors up. He will think it is me and watch where you go. I can never get away from him. While he is distracted, I will be able to get away. I know it's a lot to ask but I don't know what else I can do!"

Sue swapped her coat reluctantly. It was her favourite: navy blue wool with a fur-trimmed hood. She put on Jane's rather scruffy red anorak and pulled up the hood to hide her dark hair. Jane promised her she would return her coat and quickly wrote out the address on an old receipt.

In trepidation, Sue walked out of the store and along the street, turning her face away from the car park. She entered the fourth shop which happened to be an ice cream parlour. Surreptitiously looking back as she entered the shop, she saw Jane rushing away in the opposite direction. She bought some ice cream to take away, dithering over her choice. Vanilla or chocolate? Did it matter? She made her way to her car, taking off the hood of the coat and exposing her hair as she walked, not wishing to be confronted by Jane's irate husband. She noticed a car across the car park take off in a hurry. Shaking, she made her way home.

Over the next few days, Sue wondered how Jane was and if she would hear from her again, and if she would ever see her coat again.

Several weeks later, Sue found a brown paper parcel on her doorstep containing her coat and a letter. On a piece of lined paper torn out of a notepad, the letter read:

Thank you for your help that day. I was desperate but not for the reasons I gave. You were so kind I feel I need to come clean. I was not hiding from my husband. I was hiding from the store security. I had already stashed the stuff I had taken in one of the cubicles in the toilets, but they were on to me. Changing clothes with you meant I could retrieve it and make my escape. I am sorry to have involved you and I felt the least I could do was to return your lovely coat, just for old times' sake.

By the way, the stuff about my husband was true. He was a violent, controlling man. He is dead now. Had a nasty accident, tripped and fell down the stairs.

Jane x

Sue sat down, still holding on to her coat and the letter. She sighed and thought, *I never did get the knickers, but the ice cream was nice.*

Out of the Darkness

Kate Stanley

She couldn't remember how she came to be there or how long she had been lying there in the dark. In fact, she wasn't really sure where she was at all. She could just about hear people talking but their unfamiliar voices were muffled and she didn't know how to attract their attention. Her throat and vocal cords seemed to have seized up.

She couldn't move her head, but if she screwed her eyes up she could just about make out some numbers moving on a digital display. She must be in the cupboard under the stairs! Had she come in to read the meter? It was in such an awkward place. Whoever designed that? Or maybe she'd gone in to find her wellingtons for the walk across the fields to school? Oh God, the children! If it was dark already, then she should have collected them from school. They should be safely home, having their tea and learning their spellings.

Panicking, she tried even harder to call out but it felt like she was drowning and no sound would come out. She tried to summon all her strength to raise an arm but it felt weighted down and was impossible to move. She could just make out people moving around her now; why wouldn't they help her?

Thinking of Rosie and Will, waiting at school for her or, God forbid, trying to walk home on their own in the dark, tears pricked the back of her eyes and she finally let out an audible, plaintive sob.

Then a soothing voice told her to relax, everything

would be OK, and someone gently took hold of her hand. The digital display stopped its furious flashing and instead emitted a comforting, rhythmic beep.

"She's back with us," the doctor declared, clearly relieved. "Well done, everyone."

Up The Junction

Garry Giles

It was coming up for 'reading week' at Aberdeen University, as it was at most others. The students had a chance to go home if they wanted to, as it was like an informal half-term, and Sally really wanted to. She missed Cornwall and her parents' home on the edge of Bodmin Moor. Even though there would be a twelve-hour train journey to deal with, she knew that even that encumbrance would be worth it. Walking to Aberdeen station she was prepared for her 'gulp' at the price of the ticket, even with student discount. Little did she know what her long journey would become!

Sally's journey would involve a change at Edinburgh but that was after three hours and she knew that she would have a table and Wi-Fi so that she could work. Also, it was likely she would have four seats to herself. She was studying Media and Communication and was a sports fanatic and her dream job would be managing communications for the ATP (Association of Tennis Professionals) tour, and consequently travelling around the world with them. That said, she would not mind which sport she started in, even if it was one that she was not familiar with. She would learn about it. It would be a foot in the door, she believed.

The train was there as expected. It was the first journey of the day. *I'll bet the driver for this leg will be back at home and will have had their tea before I have even arrived,* she thought, then settled down behind a table with three spare seats and room to spread out. She was trying to write an article about the Roland-Garros grand slam tournament to submit to their online magazine. Again, a possible foot in the door.

As the train drew nearer to Scotland's east coast Sally was distracted by the views. From Montrose to Arbroath was particularly picturesque. At Montrose you can just see the people on the lovely beach, some even daring to wade into the ever cold North Sea. *Brave people*, she thought, remembering the warm Cornish waters. Then to Arbroath and the desire to smell the 'smokies' cooking. Sally had been to a restaurant there once as a birthday treat from a friend and had the most beautiful haddock she had ever tasted. She could almost taste it now, as well as the roasted tomatoes and crab dumplings that they were served with. What a happy memory.

She went back to work for a while before the excitement of travelling over the Forth rail bridge. *What an extraordinary piece of engineering it is*, she thought, *and covering a vast expanse of water. Even the aeroplanes taking the sharp turn to Edinburgh airport look as though they may dip a wing in the water! Better get myself sorted,* she thought to herself, as she needed to change trains, and the next leg was nine hours!

Once again it was the starting point for the train, though 'Cross Country' trains have narrower seats and a bit less leg room. Not a problem though, thought Sally, as she had her large holdall up on the luggage shelf. She settled into her seat; this time with a new book to read. She knew that the ride to the border would have little interest for her, even from her window seat, and there weren't any other passengers to fascinate her either. She relaxed and read for the next hour or so.

At Berwick-upon-Tweed, the world seemed to open again as she saw the mouth of the river and the bridge towering over it; and once again the sea was a backdrop on her left-hand side. Trundling on, Sally had promised herself that one day she would stop at Alnwick as she had heard that it was a wonderful place to go walking. Then came Newcastle! The platform was packed, and suddenly so was the train too. Sally closed her eyes, pretending to be asleep, as she could hear a rowdiness that she really did not want to witness. Apparently, they were on their way to Leeds to watch a football match. Sally decided to keep her head down and try and have a snooze for the hour and a bit that this part would take.

At Leeds there was an outpouring of people, though many others joined too; and three of them sat at her table. Two of them seemed to be travelling with a lot of luggage: not only their suitcases, but they also seemed to have a projector and a flip chart pad as well! There wasn't really room for their suitcases, so they put them in the vestibule where the toilet with an automatic door was. They had to keep checking on them because of the movement of the train and their wheeled cases moved around a lot. At least Sally had something to laugh about. They were up and down all the time checking their cases and teasing people on their way to the toilet who asked if it was free. Even if they knew someone was in there but had not locked the door, they would say it was free, and a very embarrassed person sitting on the toilet would be there for all to see! The door did not close quickly. Sally thought it strange that so many people would make that mistake until she realised that they tapped a shoe against the door as it was closing, and it seemed to stop the message of 'engaged' working properly. Oh well: they got off at Birmingham, and she was now nearly halfway home.

The rest of the journey was now mostly inland although she wanted to be awake for when the train left Exeter and travelled along the South Devon coastline, especially by

Dawlish where the sea would be right at her side, but she was in a deep sleep by now.

When she awoke Sally was in the sidings at Plymouth, though she did not realise that. For her it was just dark and there was only silence. How would she get to Bodmin Moor now? Most urgently she was desperate to go to the loo. The light on her phone showed her where the toilet was but it was operated electrically, and everything was turned off so the door would not open. She remembered what she had seen earlier and tapped her shoe on the bottom of the door: it opened! She was looking for a foot in the door in her career, but this was the best one she had ever experienced to date.

I Don't Know You, Don't I?

Richard Hounsfield

A true story...

THIRTY YEARS AGO

Wow, what a surprise!

"Hi!" I said.

Steve turned as I strode expectantly towards him, my hand outstretched.

"What are you doing here?" I asked.

Steve replied, "Hi," but looked blank.

I gamely followed with, "How are you?"

He was unrecognising and my mind fuzzed into confusion. It wasn't like he wanted to ignore me; it was like he didn't know me. This was a strange and disconcerting encounter.

Disorientation rippled down from head to foot as my sense of 'self' evaporated. As I shook his uncertain palm, it was the weirdest feeling to be holding my friend's hand while he looked straight through me without a flicker of friendship.

This was a freakishly unsettling experience and I was bemused.

THIRTY-THREE YEARS AGO

Ravenswood was the most brilliant live music hangout ever! Hidden away in 'designated-driver' territory miles from anywhere was an old country pile that hosted bands because Steve loved music. His family had built the wealth that he now inhabited and for an affordable price we could get in and feel like part of some exclusive Ravenswood gang, spending far too long at the bar, tapping away to solo singer-songwriters or moshing to James Brown funk bands like The Blunter Brothers, still going today, to full-on rockers like Steamhouse, sadly not still going today.

The main room was cavernous with a high ceiling, ornate wooden staircases and balconies, oak panels boasting coats of arms, and a grand ancient fireplace saturated with smoky musical history. Sometimes there were five of us and sometimes one hundred and fifty-five – those were the best nights, packed with hot energy and no reason to go home.

I made sure that I was Steve's friend; knowing the landlord is always a great insurance policy for the late lock-in. It was always the same deal after hours: landlord pours, punter pays, everyone drinking happily, slurring through band dissections while blurrily propping up the wooden bar and never remembering what time we were politely booted out.

THIRTY YEARS AGO (continued...)

I hadn't been to Ravenswood for six months because Steve had called it a day. He couldn't afford the upkeep on the stately old house so the gigs stopped as the sale signs went up. We were gutted.

So now here I was at a country fayre beer festival speaking at Steve.

"Hi! What are you doing here? How are you?"

And then the cold blankness.

As he hesitantly accepted my offered hand, he replied, "Richard."

"Yes!"

At last, what a relief, he's recognised me.

"Hi, how are you?" I said again.

But the unflinching stare of non-recognition wilted me, again. He looked at me, but my friend didn't *know* me.

"Yes, Richard. It's Richard, you know..." I self-consciously trailed, searching desperately for a flicker of something, anything.

Now Steve looked really confused, dryly stating, "My name is Richard."

What? Suspended in seconds of internal panic as I searched for sense, and then liberation for both of us from the prison of puzzlement as Richard added flatly, "My brother's name is Steve."

It was only then that I dimly remembered Steve describing his troubled relationship with his brothers, particularly his identical twin brother, with Ravenswood being the heart of the issue. I was meeting Steve's estranged twin brother, Richard, and he was meeting his estranged twin brother's friend, Richard.

As the penny dropped on this weird identity crisis, we were both a tad traumatised and suddenly awkward, and after a few meaningless pleasantries, we left in opposite directions.

It Was Christmas Eve

Lisbeth Cameron

This was the Christmas I spent in a confined space.

It was Christmas Day, the biggest event of the year. I suddenly noticed that the kitchen sink was blocked. In desperation I crawled in under the sink to see what could be done to improve the situation. I presumed it would involve unscrewing the U-shaped bend in the pipe. I manoeuvred my upper body into the small place – and got stuck.

To make things worse the small mouse trap, which was placed in the corner, was now just in front of my face! In my horror I imagined spending the rest of the evening in this most uncomfortable position which was slowly getting to be a painful posture. My bottom was in the air outside, and one knee was inside underneath me, completely preventing me from moving forward or backwards. At this rate, our guests would not get their dinner and I, by the time I got out, would be in such pain with a severe backache that no dinner would be served anyway.

The plan was to unscrew the pipe and let it run into a bowl underneath. But all I could do was worry about my situation and the consequences. At the moment no bowl could be passed to me and taken inside; I was simply stuck.

Should I ask someone to phone the fire brigade? My son, always full of good ideas suggested he just pull my leg to get me out. The dog, aware of something unusual, started to add to the commotion by barking excessively. I was desperate to change position and to relieve the pain in my back.

If I let my head go downwards it would get too close to the mouse trap. My husband started to fill up everyone's glasses to gain some time and was thinking where he could get some takeaway food. Meanwhile, the cramps and pain in my shoulders and back just got worse and worse.

The only positive thing was that there was no mouse in the trap, but my nose was very close to the danger zone. There was nothing else to do but laugh at the situation. As I was trying different methods of moving slowly backwards, I must have passed out.

When I woke up, the backache was still there, but thank goodness I was no longer under the sink!

CHAPTER 4

THE MOON AND STARS

Looking At The Moon

Moyra Zaman

I look at the moon
and marvel at my rock –
a pitted face of shadowlands,
hewn historically
and keeping time
tick-tocking at my door.

Rhythmical certainty
concertinas round
my meagre life;
a centrifugal waltz
of wax and wanes –
a mystical delight.

Fine flirting sliver,
winking down
at dusky days
transitioning to night –
a cautious crescent
of glowing reflected light.

I watch the blossoming
of moonbeam hours
mature to opalescence;
magnificently ripe,
a crisply conjured sphere
overseeing the night.

Silent recipient of my
wavering thoughts,
registering the ebb and flow
of turbulent dreams,
and anchoring the wayward sighs
of restless souls in space.

A watchful companion,
my confidant and
valued go-between;
a steady sounding board,
galvanising friendships,
whispering from afar.

Occasionally obscured,
negotiating nights
of jealous clouds,
the moon reliably returns
to claim the shadows
from my heart.

Widower's Thoughts

Garry Giles

You are twinkling at me, my little star
From a long, long way away: so far
You are probably not little at all
But a shining light or a glowing ball

I have taken to looking out for you
In the evening rain, it is still what I do
You see, I think I know just who you are
My nightly visitor, my twinkling star

I wonder in the day if you contact me too
For strange things appear looking up to the blue
Could be contrails where planes cross when they fly
Maybe it's you sending a kiss in the sky

Twinkle again tonight my little star
I will never forget you and all that you are
Fifty years we spent together
Kisses and twinkles keep you alive forever.

The Beauty Of Nature And Stillness

Lisbeth Cameron

I love going out late at night with my dog to make her run around for the last business before going to bed. The garden in this lockdown is extremely quiet, a stillness I have never noticed before. One could say that the stillness in all its quietness actually seems noisy in the ears. Some say it is the body responding to the 'no noise'.

I just stand there enjoying the quiet with the dark sky above. The trees can be seen as dark silhouettes against the lighter sky. I am just living and savouring the moment. Maybe reflecting on the day's happenings. The dog just sniffs around finding the very best spot to use.

And then I saw the moon. Sitting low on the horizon with its full circular shape in clear contrast to the sky, giving light to us humans on the ground. Can you see there is a face in the moon? I can clearly see a surprised face with a mouth puckered in amazement over all the things the moon can see happening down here. I have tried to draw the face several times, copying the shadows accurately, but I can't make it look like the face I see. Furthermore, I have never come across a drawing that looks like what I see. So maybe no one else can see it.

No wonder the moon is surprised, considering all the superstition and ignorance it must be watching. It is not made of blue cheese, and it cannot interfere in our lives. Or maybe it can: just think of the tides coming and going all over the world.

The constant waning and waxing changing every two weeks, has always been a puzzle for human beings. Interesting enough it was first described in 1300. If the crescent is open to the left the moon is waxing and if the opening is to the right, the moon is waning. That is another puzzle to remember.

I take a deep breath at all this beauty surrounding me and realise the dog has done what it came to do. So, we go in for a night's sleep.

An Eye On The World

Kate Stanley

In the western sky at sunset a vesper star looks down, a heavenly body with its eye on the world. Ever-present yet long gone, there are countless light-years between us. Just a luminous ball of gas, yet something special and celestial.

This stellar presence, shining bright with 20/20 vision, has seen it all. It was a silent witness to first life emerging, spluttering from the sea. It watched the giant steps of dinosaurs, and the first pterodactyl flights. Later, it saw early man rising shakily onto two feet, the first scratchings on cave walls, the first flickering light of flinty fire.

This all-seeing eye watched the Greeks on Mount Olympus and the Romans crowned with laurel. It has seen the night sky mapped and studied, and ancient Chinese dynasties rise and fall like white dwarves. This was the star that led eastern kings on ships of the desert towards a humble stable, where a baby cried. And when a messiah died, cloudy cataracts passed over this eye.

Cold and glinting, it looked on as deadly plague afflicted the land and then as London blazed. It watched the elegant sweep of crinolines around marbled halls, while ragged boys climbed chimneys, their mothers sweating in dark mills.

Silently it observes but does not judge, even the self-destruction of two world wars, and countless more. It has seen men look up from bleak trenches, praying to be back home again, while sweethearts long for a letter but dread a telegram.

The eye on the world has seen it all, witnessed birth and death, invention and destruction in equal measure; man's intelligence used to build and to tear down.

Now our star notes the melting ice caps, the choking oceans, the flooding valleys and another plague, yet still it rises, shimmering in the evening sky, encouraging the world to look up and hope.

Star

Emma Barratt

In my garden, standing cold, uncontrolled yet bold,
Tired of being locked in, waiting as I grow old,
Soothing green mud-bathed grass beneath my feet,
A small red-brick home behind, my family seat.

I have escaped, so breathe deep and look for a light,
Find nothing but curtains drawn, no warmth in sight.
The glistening black crab apple scratches the sky,
A cushy cloud collective sinks beneath the last appley eye.

Unflinching fusion, heat glowing, my beloved flashing
pearl,
Exploding light-years away, a mystery to unfurl,
Blinds my corner eye, this gorgeous gas made flare.
I am struck, only able to stand and stare.

A dashing, daring, decorated, silver rock star,
Co-operating for a map of life, a navigating north star.
My burning hydrogen helium celestial heart, so far away,
Eternally above this bawdy patch of England, waiting to
play.

My bright star glows down upon me and seems to want to
say,
He depends on me. Find me! "I am here across the Milky
Way."
Waiting for my response, I am dismayed to my core,
Twinkling for me, so far away, a tragic cry, I can only ignore.

I return to the safety of my soft, safe home,
Leaving my 'object of astronomy' free, eternally to roam.
I slip quietly, purposefully, peacefully into my bed,
to dream, to encounter the splendid, shimmering star,
somewhere in my head.

Lunar Reflections

Kate Stanley

For millennia our silent, inscrutable moon has risen and set as predictably as the sun; ever present, bright at night, a cloudy cataract in the daytime sky. Over a lunar month her thin crescent appears first in the west, waxes to luminous fullness then wanes to a thin silver sliver again in the eastern sky just before dawn. Together with the sun she drags the weight of the earth's water in her gravitational pull, causing mighty oceans to rise and fall in a tidal ritual.

This celestial object, our nearest neighbour in space, wears a cloak of myth and mystery. Hanging in the heavens she is driven across the night sky by Selene, Goddess of the Moon. She is the depository of our ancestral memory, protector and guardian of our earth. Worshipped by pagans, she exerts her lunatic power over werewolves. Her Seas of Tranquility and Serenity are fantastic destinations of imagination, though lava is the only liquid that ever lapped their rocky shores.

So it was that for years the moon was magical in my mind's eye, until that summer's day fifty years ago. Then I looked at the moon and thought, *Why?* Why did they have to go there and trample its virgin surface with their weighted lunar boots? Why did they have to plant a flag of ownership, as if it was the 51st state of America? That giant leap for mankind has diminished the majestic moon, pedestrianised her.

Knowledge and disappointment have replaced wonder, for now we know that our beautiful silver satellite is lifeless and dusty. The vast moonscape of rough, grey rubble is like crumbling mortar on an ancient edifice. There are no geodes bursting with amethyst, no emeralds in the seas or opals in the craters. The Sea of Tranquility is a giant dustbowl in a silent grey wasteland. The moon's mystery has evaporated, but unaware of this she rises and sets, waxes and wanes, and the ocean still holds up a mirror to her beauty.

CHAPTER 5

IMAGINATION AND ADVENTURE

A Midsummer Dream

Sarah-Jane Reeve

I dreamt I was walking but suddenly, I felt dread. What about home? Had I left the front door open? A restless breeze blew leaves towards me and among them I saw paper masks. I retraced my steps along the track.

The front door was wide open, and written on it were my passwords for all to see.

"Hello," I called, but there was only silence.

I climbed stairs carpeted in fading equations and headlines: R is up to 20. My family was gone. The floors were littered with banknotes and air tickets.

The cat looked up from her quarantine on the bookcase; her eyes were moonbeams and the books were unread. She meowed but the sound was the rustle of a million leaves. She climbed into my arms and realising there were no goodbyes we ran to the waiting trees.

Deep in the wood I knew it was all over. Breathing freely, soothed by birdsong. At the oak tree I pulled back the blanket of moss. I lay down in the earth like a seed and the falling leaves covered me. The trees sighed.

"Stay," they said. "You can be rooted and still touch the sky."

*

Hunt the Rainbow

Lorraine Surridge

A s far as the admiralty knew for sure, the *Sea Kist* was a whaling ship that had been roaming the seas for her bounty for the last six months. Recently, however, admiralty spies had sent disturbing news that whaling was her cover, and that she was really spying on the Royal Navy for the French, Spanish and Dutch. Indeed, she would spy for anyone who was prepared to pay her going price, as it was believed that the captain of the *Sea Kist* was not partisan and would sell information about any fleet to the highest bidder. This belief had growing credence due to eyewitness reports that the crew of the *Sea Kist* were never short of doubloons whenever, and wherever, they made port. Certainly, there was very little evidence of her bringing whale blubber, spermaceti or ambergris into any of the main ports in the region. Each of these whale products was in high demand and could make their crew a great profit, so suspicions were rife about the source of their wealth, if it was not from whaling. Of course, piracy was the alternative, but with the nous of her wily captain and the loyalty of his crew, she hadn't been caught at that either.

Today those suspicions were going to be verified. At eight bells the ship's company of HMS *Dido* were preparing to board the whaling schooner *Sea Kist*. As the *Dido* was approaching the *Sea Kist* under the cloak of a sea mist, luck was not on their side. With the mist rapidly dissipating it was threatening to ruin their element of surprise.

Just as the *Dido*'s Captain Exelby was about to give the

order to pull alongside, the lookout from the *Sea Kist* called, "Thar she blows," and the *Sea Kist* swiftly turned into the wind and pulled away from HMS *Dido* at a phenomenal speed. Being swifter and more manoeuvrable than *Dido* they had no chance of keeping up with her.

"Avast," Captain Exelby called to cease the *Dido*'s planned course of action.

As he did so a voice drifted towards him on the wind, and he heard the command of the captain of the *Sea Kist* to his helmsman, "Hunt for the rainbow."

Looking into the distance through his spyglass, Captain Exelby could see a series of long wispy rainbows caused by the spray from the blowhole of a large breaching whale refracting on the light of the oncoming dawn. Overlapping arches of red, orange, yellow, green, blue, indigo and violet filled the sky.

Captain Exelby bit his lip and paced the poop deck in frustration as he announced to his first mate, "Sadly we will have to report in the ship's log, that the *Sea Kist* is a whaler after all."

And with that, he descended to his cabin to write his daily report.

In the distance, as the *Sea Kist* was bearing down on the location of the rainbow, the lookout shouted to its captain that HMS *Dido* was retreating.

Cheers went up from the *Sea Kist* as the crew made ready to change direction to continue on their planned journey to Port Royal where they would meet up with other pirates. That lucky whale would live to swim the seas for another day, and in a few hours, the crew of the *Sea Kist* would be drinking to their own lucky escape.

The Wardrobe Lockdown

Moyra Zaman

Some called it a wardrobe, others, a home,
a posh penitentiary is how it was known.
Inexplicably hurt, I came to be here
for a day, or a week, a month, now a year!
I slithered between the old-timers' stares,
squirmed at their wrinkles while crushing their layers.
I'd upset the pecking order, for sure –
it upset me – it was hard to endure.

Uncomfortably cramped and jostling for space,
I came face to face with a bosom of lace,
flaunting itself and seeking affection.
Then a buttoned-up jerkin's disdainful inspection
revealed how at odds we all were with each other;
some liked exposure, some crouched under cover,
some crumpled and fell in a heap with the shoes,
unfashionably proud and sorely abused.

Some harem we were, motley and many,
always on call in case there were any
sudden demands for appropriate service;
the moment of choice left us all very nervous!

My chances were good, my designs were top rate,
in forecasted colours, I was bang up to date.
And so, I was chosen and spread on the bed,
stroked and admired, slipping over her head.
I'd escaped for the night, but I needed much more;
I lowered my standards and sank to the floor.

Soiled with its dirt and soaked with her tears,
I was sent to the cleaners; my heart cried out, 'Cheers!'

Hooking my eyes on the posh clientele,
I copied their number on to my lapel.
When the chauffeur came by to collect for the lady,
I was duly adopted and, like a new baby,
was cosseted gently and carefully installed
in a room full of mirrors from wall to wall.
No longer confined in a dark dismal pen;
I was hanging about with the best of them then!

The Hole In The Fence

Lorraine Surridge

"Grandpa, please tell me again what you saw through the hole in the fence?"

"Well now, where did we get to?"

"You were sent there to help."

"So we were. We had been diverted from our original mission and it took us three days to get there. When we arrived, well let's just say it was in the nick of time. There was devastation. Many people had lost their homes and … you're looking puzzled, what's up?"

"Was there a train? At Devas station?"

"Aha, when you say it like Grandpa, it does sound a bit like a place, but what I mean is nothing was left standing. Not a tree or a house or a school. Just rubble and wood scattered about as far as the eye could see. The only living things were people wandering about. Some standing, in a daze, others rushing frantically looking under what used to be buildings searching for belongings or friends and family lost in the earthquake. Everyone was mostly calm until... well occasionally the ground shook with aftershock tremors although the gaps in between were getting longer by the time we had got there. As I think I mentioned, on the way we had stopped off at a port to take on supplies of water, food and blankets for the islanders."

"Go on, Grandpa, tell me what you saw through the hole in the fence."

"Well now, hold your horses, I'm getting to that. So, we

were split into teams and detailed to help with either unloading supplies or building new shelters. My commander sent me out to discover where the supplies should be taken first but I needed an interpreter. That's when I found the old man by the dock, or I should say, he found me. I was expecting someone in charge. You know, a bigwig of some sort, island president or town mayor perhaps. Just when I was thinking that they must all have perished in the quake this very old man comes up to me and in perfect English he says... 'We will go now.' And with that he walks off."

"But you go with him, don't you, Grandpa?"

"Well, after some dithering about, it occurs to me that at least I had found my interpreter, so I catch up with him and we begin to walk out of what used to be the main town. In truth, my lad, I was a bit annoyed as he wouldn't give me straight answers to straight questions."

"I kept asking him: 'Where are we going?'

"'You will see'" was always his reply.

"This continued the whole time we walked. Now I say walked but a lot of it was actually climbing over and under obstructions along the way. I was a young man then but even so I found it hard going. This old man took it all in his stride. He was as thin and flexible as a skipping rope and he didn't slow down the whole hour it took to get to the fence."

"Good, finally we are at the fence. What did you see, Grandpa?"

"Yes, well what a sight it was too. With everything else completely gone this fence stood high and sturdy along the horizon. It shook me up a bit, I can tell you. It looked so out of place. I turned to ask the old man where we were but... he was gone. I felt like a complete fool. I'd been led to goodness knows where and upon my arrival had immediately lost my interpreter. Then to add insult to injury my two-way radio crackled and the not-friendly voice of my sergeant booms out... 'Where are you?'

"Good question, I thought, but obviously I didn't say that. I didn't want extra latrine duties when we got back. So, I delayed answering for a moment and walked up to the fence to get a better look. The path to the fence sloped upwards so by the time I got to the fence it wasn't quite as high as it had first looked, although still much too tall for me to see over. My radio crackled again, and a voice asked with increasing annoyance: 'Where the hell are you?'

"Finally, gathering my wits, I replied, 'Sarg, I'm on the outskirts of town reconnoitring the options for supply disbursement.'

"'Well, Roger that. And bloody well keep in touch,' came the reply.

"Confirming that I would be in touch again very soon, I continued to walk along the fence line looking for a way in. As I followed the fence along and around, I soon realised it was an enclosure; a kind of fort perhaps, but at no point could I find an entrance such as a gate or door. Just as I was considering finding a foothold to climb over, I noticed a knot hole in the fence at about knee height."

Unable to contain himself, the boy said, "Hurry up, Grandpa, tell me what you saw."

His Grandpa smiled and after a second or two he continued. "Bending down on one knee, I peeped through the knot hole in the fence and what a surprise I got. Children. As far as the eye could see. Rows and rows of children sitting cross-legged facing a large statue. 'Hello!' I shouted through the hole. But none of the children moved. 'Hello!' I shouted again. 'We have come to help.'

"Not a movement could be seen inside until what happened next gave me such a fright ... A piercing blue eyeball that penetrated my soul looked out into mine from the other side of the hole. I yelled out something unrepeatable and fell backwards. As I lay unable to move a muscle, I heard a scraping sound somewhere to my right and then movement as a section of the fence swung down like a drawbridge. I stood up and walked towards the opening trying to keep calm. Arriving at the gap in the fence I peered inside. The children were all still seated but were now looking back over their shoulders in my direction. I cautiously entered the enclosure."

Grandpa paused to take a sip of green tea that Grandma had just placed at his side. "Indeed," he continued, winking at the boy, "compared with the Devas station elsewhere, I had found a calm and beautiful oasis. I was full of wonderment at the vision before me. The dominant feature of the enclosure was the giant grey statue towering over all within and the pong coming from animals grazing in wooden enclosures behind the base of the statue. Alongside the animals were about fifty or so women stirring a liquid, contained inside twenty massive cauldrons, with huge wooden paddles over deep pits heated by burning logs. The curious thing was that still no one moved towards me. Then I realised that the children hadn't got up because they were all seated on long bamboo rafts floating gently on an emerald-green lagoon. Small white birds swam around the rafts occasionally dipping their heads under the surface. It was a surreal yet magical scene."

Grandpa paused and stared into the distance as if he was actually reliving the experience. After a minute or two he continued.

"As I took it all in, I felt a light tap on my shoulder and

turned to see a lovely apparition before me. She was as tall as me, slim, with dark brown hair and those same piercing blue eyes I had seen earlier. Once more I was mesmerised by those eyes but not in a malevolent way. She bowed her head and spoke in a melodic tone of voice in exquisite English. 'I try not to scare you this time,' looking at me and smiling mischievously. Then she answered my quizzical look. 'Oh the children and the livestock were all brought here for safety when the Father of our island, the old man who brought you here, sensed a change in the weather. Shortly afterwards we felt the first tremors. Built by his ancestors, they have used this sacred lagoon many times for safety. They come here to pray to their gods for survival of quakes and tsunamis. They say they have never failed them. They must be right as they have sent you.'

"Feeling very humbled, I remembered my mission and asked what supplies they needed, most of which amounted to water, rice, fruit, vegetables and some medicines. Communicating this back by radio to my commanding officer, I gave approximate directions from town, explaining the need to clear the roads before any truck could make the journey.

"I needn't have worried as within the hour three helicopters arrived overhead carrying provisions. Large bales of supplies were dropped first, followed by several relief personnel who abseiled down just outside the enclosure, to the excitement of the children. As the relief mission took over, a medic set up a first-aid tent and the three helicopter crews returned to base with news of the survivors. As gently as I could, I explained to the beautiful girl, whom I discovered was a schoolteacher on temporary secondment from the mainland, that the town had been completely destroyed by the quake and that, with the exception of the old man and a few helpers in town, this lagoon and everyone in it were the only people I had seen. She relayed this news to the other women. In truth I was a little surprised at the lack of an outpouring of grief. Instead, the girl returned and asked: 'They want to know how many bodies you have found in the water.'

"Taken aback by the question, I explained that we hadn't found any. She passed this news on and the women and children all clapped and cheered. Seeing my confused expression, the girl took my arm and said, 'I see you don't understand. This is an island nation of fishermen. When we came here for safety the men took their boats and sailed away beyond danger so they could return and provide for their families. Hopefully, they will see them sail back safely in the next day or so.'

"And that," Grandpa concluded, "was exactly what happened. Over the next seven days as my fellow crewmen helped clear away the debris and dug foundations for, new, more robust buildings, the fishermen returned. Mostly one or two each day, with one magnificent day when about thirty small boats appeared over the horizon carrying ninety islanders in total. Each evening the islanders prayed and gave thanks to their gods that in time they would recover and live happily together once more."

"And they did, didn't they Grandpa? All live happily ever after."

"Well, I'm sure some did," said Grandpa, gazing dreamily into the piercing blue eyes of the little boy's grandma.

Another Time

Joyce Smith

It was a lot more spacious in there than I had imagined. It could, in fact, be termed a walk-in wardrobe, although no such thing existed in the days when the house was built. It was called 'The Old House' in the holiday brochure and it lived up to its name.

On entering the wardrobe, in the bedroom I had decided was to be mine, I was surprised to see another door facing me. As I was contemplating this, I heard the door behind me click closed. I looked for a handle or catch on the inside of the door to allow my escape. I called to my children who were excitedly exploring their rooms, but they obviously could not hear me. I looked around for some other way out and noticed faint light leaking around the strange inner door. Pulling away the cobwebs, I noticed it had a substantial padlock. Out of curiosity, I jiggled the padlock in a half-hearted manner when, to my surprise, it came away in my hand. Cautiously opening the door, I found old wooden stairs in a bad state of repair. Having made another failed attempt to summon help, I decided to follow the stairs down to where they led, into a small faintly lit area with a stone floor.

Unsteadily I made my way down the rickety steps. I thought I could hear voices and I could make out another door at the bottom of the stairs. I opened it cautiously and with difficulty and was precipitated out into bright sunshine. I was astonished to find myself in a marketplace. Not the usual kind of marketplace. It looked as if people were selling goods randomly, either on the ground or from carts. There seemed to be no proper stalls or designated places. Rushes were spread underneath the stalls to keep their wares away from the dirt floor. People were dressed in clothes from long ago. They were selling bread, cheese, eggs, vegetables, fruit and clothing. There were chickens and pigs which added to the cacophony of sound from the market traders. Looking around, I tried to understand what I was seeing. My immediate thought was that the whole thing was a theatrical re-enactment of a time long gone by. I was thinking how authentic it all was when I heard the name 'Joan' shouted again and again. From behind an arm grasped mine and a cheerful girl peered into my face.

"Where 'ave you been? I've been looking for you everywhere."

I looked down at the arm grasping mine and realised with a shock that I was dressed in similar garb to everyone else there: a rough homespun skirt and top covered with a coarse apron. I could feel the dirt underneath my feet and knew I had no shoes on. Not only that but I knew the girl's name. She was called Betsy and she was my sister. Confused, I allowed myself to be led across the market square towards a makeshift stall on a cart that was selling eggs and chickens.

"Joan, where've you been?" moaned the woman standing behind the stall. "I've been really busy."

I stared at her. With a shock I knew that I recognised her. I knew she was my mother. The next few hours were spent with my brain in turmoil, helping the woman on the stall, selling eggs, the occasional chicken, some vegetables and rough home-made clothing. It seemed to be expected of me. Strangely, I accepted the fact that she was my mother, and I knew her name was Martha, the same way I knew Betsy was my sister. Disorientated, I just set about doing what, surprisingly, seemed to be second nature to me. I had no time to think.

It was a long day. Eventually, tired and dirty, we made our long way home to what could only be described as a hovel. Nevertheless, I was pleased to see it. After bread and a kind of thin vegetable soup for supper, I fell, exhausted, into a bed I shared with my sisters, Betsy and Kate.

I woke up at the crack of dawn with the crowing of the cock. I lay still so as not to wake my sisters and tried to puzzle out my situation only to be summoned almost immediately by my mother to go and feed the chickens. As the days went by, I realised that with my growing acceptance of the family and surroundings, I was less and less able to recount my previous life. It all seemed so normal. Every day for the next week was the same. Getting up at dawn. Feeding the chickens and collecting the eggs. Mucking out the pigsty and tending to the meagre vegetable crop on our tiny bit of land or foraging in the woods and hedgerows for berries and edible plants. Most of the time, we girls had to do the hard stuff as our father went fishing to supplement our food. As the days turned into weeks, I had begun to accept this way of life, until, after four weeks, market day arrived again.

It was still dark when we loaded up the cart with chickens and eggs, a few homespun aprons and any vegetables we could spare. We made the long journey into town, taking it in turn to ride on the cart. By the time we got there, we were dusty, hungry and thirsty. Our mother handed out pieces of bread, and then sent me off to the well with a pitcher to fetch refreshment for everyone. No one liked going to the pump. It was situated in the old part of the square by the aptly named 'The Old House'. It was rumoured demonic practices had taken place there, many years ago, when it was occupied. Frightened people had reported ghostly noises coming from the building.

I planned to fill the pitcher as quickly as I could and make my way back, but, as I neared the pump, I could hear other voices apart from the general market noise and realised with much consternation that they seemed to be coming from the haunted house. There was a porch, mostly obscured by ivy and hidden in the porch was a door. The voices seemed to be coming from there. I was very frightened and turned to run away but the voices, louder now, sounded familiar and I was drawn back. As I approached, I could hear shouting. Someone was calling. I opened the door as if in a trance and climbed with much trepidation up the rotten stairs. I hesitated and opened the door at the top. Again, I heard someone calling. My son stood at the open door of the wardrobe.

"Mum, where have you been?" he said excitedly. "We want to show you our rooms. Can we go to the beach after?"

A Different Place

Lorraine Surridge

Another day just like any other was about to begin. She felt the warmth of the rising sun heating up the kitchen as its rays crept in through the open door and spread like tentacles across the bare wooden floorboards. The rest of the Kindred in the Idyll were still asleep but somewhere outside, in the distance, she could hear seasonal workers arriving who had come to coppice the nearby forest. Soon the sound of chainsaws would replace the birdsong she so enjoyed, which had become the only highlight of her day.

Her back still ached from yesterday's work of collecting all the fallen tree nuts. Today her task was to crack open the nuts, pickle and bottle them for the Kindred winter larder. As Leaf scooped the broken walnut shells into a bowl, she found herself overwhelmed with a feeling of deep sadness. Outside, the chainsaws had yet to start but interwoven with the morning birdsong she could hear the strains of a long-forgotten tune. A country music song that had been part of her old life. A family favourite, sung together on long car journeys on past happy family holidays. It must have been playing on the radio belonging to one of the forest workers. Members of the Kindred were not allowed any electrical equipment as it may "infect" the Idyll.

Leaf stood spellbound as the words from the song reached her ears. Without meaning to, she began to mouth the words as the song continued.

Staring down at her hands Leaf was suddenly alarmed at how her fingertips resembled the very pickled walnuts she was pickling. Every day had become as dreary as the chore she was undertaking. Why was she living a life of servitude rather than the blissful tranquillity promised all those years ago. With despair she realised it had actually been seven summers since she had joined the Kindred. In the first few years she had been at the centre of the life of the Chosen one, then, as her teenage youth faded, so did his interest in her. Now she washed, cooked, cleaned and generally skivvied from daybreak until all candlelight had been extinguished.

The song had finished, and Leaf stood frozen on the cusp of a dilemma. It was heartbreaking to realise that she no longer belonged at the Idyll as well as soul destroying to feel so lost. What was there to live for?

Once more the strains of another song floated across to her and the tears began to roll down her cheeks. The voice sang as if he was in the same room. Increasingly aware of a presence she turned around, and there he was, singing to her as he had done when she was his little girl, his sweet Caroline. Not Leaf, but Caroline.

She couldn't find the words, but her father spoke for both of them.

"Looks to me like we're ready to go home."

Sobbing uncontrollably Caroline walked out of the kitchen into the sunlight without looking back, her sagging shoulders cradled by her father.

The psychiatrist had been right. "Keep trying; one day she will become disillusioned with the cult and that is when she will be ready to return with you." This had been her father's eighth attempt to reach her with music from her childhood. On the long drive home her father continued to play the mixtape, afraid that if it stopped it would break the spell and she would once more return to the controlling influence of the Idyll. He had been warned that undoing the indoctrination would take time, but he had seen that the old Caroline was still in there and at this moment that was enough.

The Whimsical Wood

Richard Hounsfield

She hurried down the path to get away from them, but who are they? And are they getting closer? Lily Rose knew she had to go but Mummy always called when she was having the most fun. Sooo annoying. But today she was glad when she heard, "Lil-leee, teee-time!"

They had lived in this little woodland paradise nestled in the Chiltern Hills for half of Lily's six years. She didn't know it was late spring because when you're six you don't really know what a season is, you just know that the sun is shining, it feels warm again after all that cold and rain, the flowers' buds are reaching up to pop their colourful gifts and you see squirrels excitedly flitting between the trees. She lived in a little cottage in an enchanted wood with Mummy. They had a small and beautifully tended garden with twenty-one separate paving stones dotted away from the cottage along the centre of the lawn to the rickety little garden gate. Lily had learned to gaily traverse the stones with eleven precise hops. You're not allowed to miss otherwise you have to start again, which meant that she could spend the first ten minutes just getting to the rickety gate. Sometimes she just sneaked a misstep and mischievously hopped from grass to the next stone hoping that the woodland fairies wouldn't notice.

Once beyond the gate the magical bluebell fairyland opened up before Lily, the path clear as if she were a tiny pixie skipping through a big blue pond. The gentle breeze ruffled the leaf-feathers of the giant protective beech trees, creating a pretty scene of dancing dappled light. Daffodils mingled with the cowslips just across the way from the extrovert show of the huge grandstanding cream cow parsley. Lily knew that's where the elves lived, neighbours to the untrustworthy goblins who ate all the puffball fungi.

Mummy had told Lily all about the fairies, elves, imps, nymphs, goblins and trolls. She had never seen any but she knew they were there. As she scampered and twirled around the circular path towards the singing stream, she saw the first brave bunnies daring to venture out for teatime nibbles. Sometimes the scaredy-cat muntjacs that might grow into Santa's reindeer if they could only not be so scared, accidentally appeared before bolting in fright at Lily's shrieks of delight. The little patches of worn earth along the path were where the forest fairies held their meetings, flying in from their tree-homes with fairy-dust twinkling in their wake. Oh how she wished she could go to one of the secret fairy meetings.

Mummy had shown her the wild blackberries so she picked a few, sometimes squidging them too hard in her fingers so Mummy would have to clean her dress, again. The fresh clear stream was a good place to swish her pink-stained hands as she imagined the frog-chatter being carried downstream by the babbling brook.

"Lil-leee, teee-time!"

She sprang upwards. The birds startled into the air, birdsong giving way to flapping wings of warblers, blackbirds and blue tits darting from the ferns to nest holes in giant trunks, a distant cuckoo falling silent.

As Lily Rose came around the last bend and the garden gate beckoned she stopped suddenly. What was that? Shadows of fairies? Too big. The delicate wood nymphs? Nobody ever sees them. She'd heard about the frightening trolls, one of them nearly ate three billy goats called "Gruff". Or maybe it was the shady goblins, she didn't want to meet them. Lily panted for breath as she ran to the safety of the rickety garden gate. She hurried down the path to get away from them, but who are they? And are they getting closer?

CHAPTER 6

THE CHILTERNS

A Random Dash Through The Chilterns

Kate Stanley

Chesham, Fingest, Flackwell Heath
Lacey Green and Cobblers Pits
Pishill, Pitstone, Winchmore Hill
Missendens, Chalfonts, Speen.

Bryant's Bottom, Walter's Ash
Weston Turville, Sharpenhoe
Dunsmore, Naphill, Nettlebed
Ellesborough, Edlesborough, Tring.

Pulpit Hill and Clipper Down
Buckland Common, Captain's Wood
Shiplake, Prestwood, Hambleden
Ibstone, Ivinghoe, Penn.

Christmas Common, Ballinger
Drayton Beauchamp, Wiggington
Bledlow Ridge and Ashley Green
Latimer, Lane End, Frieth.

Hyde Heath, South Heath, Amersham
Chartridge, Hawridge, Bottom Wood
Aston Clinton, Saunderton
Coleshill, Naphill, Thame.

In The Chilterns

Garry Giles

It was the summer of 1983 when I first arrived in Chesham. I was 24 and busy with a career. Having grown up in North London, and now living in South London, countryside was a holiday thing. Wherever I had lived, you only knew that you were in a different town because the postcode changed on the street names. So why was I on this train travelling to the very top left corner of the London Underground map?

A dear friend of mine, who I had known since our first day at infants' school, had become a train driver and said that he was moving to Chesham, as he was changing from working on the deep underground, to the Metropolitan Line, and this would be easier for him. He was buying a house in White Hill, sold by 'Chiltern Estates', who themselves resided at the bottom of White Hill on the corner of the High Street, and asked me if I would go with him to have a look.

The train (destined for Amersham) seemed to race through what was known as 'Metroland', but then after Rickmansworth everything changed. All of a sudden I could see open land, and not just a piece of land: acres and acres of it. It would go on. At Chalfont and Latimer station we had to change on to the Chesham 'shuttle' for the single-track ride to our destination.

The ride on this half-length train was so unexpected. We were high up looking across gorgeous Chiltern countryside on what was the most winding journey I had probably ever experienced on a train. Then, as we approached Chesham station very slowly, I saw three things (though I did not know their names at the time): the steep hill of Lowndes Park to my left; another steep hill this time to Dungrove Farm on my right; and, when we stepped off the train, Nashleigh Hill ahead. I told my friend that I would like to live here too. No need for postcodes on the street names, here the countryside defined borders.

We looked at his house between Kirtle Road and Broadlands Avenue, and then set off on a walk: my very first walk in the Chilterns.

On the other side of White Hill there is a path that climbs high up and we ventured over a stile and, after walking upwards for a while, we happened upon that Dungrove Farm I had seen on our arrival. We then made our way along a footpath in the fields; the views were stunning. Eventually striding down to a roughly made road (Bottom Lane), we could see what looked like a pub not too far away. By now we needed some lunch. We arrived at what was then called The Five Bells, and were both welcomed and well fed. Later returning the same way, as we had no idea how to get there by road, we made our way back to the station to start our different journeys home.

I had witnessed and enjoyed the Chilterns for the first time, and I vowed to move here, and I did so a few years later in 1987. Over the last 34 years I have enjoyed many pleasurable walks and local places.

I love London and would still describe it as the best city in the world, but the Chilterns are such a delight. In addition, during my time here, Red Kites have become a beautiful feature of our skies. Inevitably there have been less positive changes, and undoubtedly there will be more to come, but what we have on our doorstep is amazing. My first memory of arriving on the train to be greeted by the Chilterns can never be erased.

A Walk With Restorative Powers

Lisbeth Cameron

The toil of my everyday life
in my soul is deeply in strife.
To survive I must have fresh air
I find my well-known boots to wear.

The wind around my cheeks will bite,
the thoughts will through my head take flight.
Walking the land of wood and plain
until the pulse has cleared my brain.

The horizon is hanging low
and by my boot the river flows.
On my path I meet a moorhen,
I begin to feel good again.

I see the deer, I hear the birds,
Clearly the sky shows me these words:
Into your lungs inhale the air,
be to yourself and nature fair.

I wander off, I wander on
before I know the day has gone.
I feel refreshed in mind and soul
and will again take up my goal.

Step Back In Time

Lorraine Surridge

Nearing the summit, a light breeze ripples through my hair. With every step I feel the energy of nature envelop me, rejuvenate me, transport me back to times gone by. My walk along this well-trodden path has led all manner of folk before me to their destination. I pass alongside banks of earth formed into lynchets through centuries of Chiltern hillside ploughing. For generations this has been a route to school, work, prayer or muster. The peace of my surroundings is interrupted by distant chimes and I picture the gatherings summoned by those same bells across the centuries. A celebration for days such as Michaelmas or Catterns. Or perhaps a dawn call to muster accompanied by men riding high atop snorting horses waving their goodbyes to mothers, wives or sweethearts bearing faces streaked with salty tears.

On this lockdown morning I approach the wood and hear the throng of birdsong competing high in the canopy. It stops abruptly as I take my first step into the wood. I, too, stop and wait. The signal is given as one bird restarts its trill song as if to announce, "Carry on, no threat detected." Serenaded, I continue deeper into this wooden realm. With every step I kick up the soft bedding underfoot of rotting flora and fauna, causing heady aromas. A few steps on I stumble on a hidden root, disturbing the industrious peace of worm and woodlouse. All my senses are alive. I twitch around at every rustle; I peer skyward at signs of movement as birds flit their nests and squirrels leap through the air on their foraging journey. Onward I step, deeper into the wood where there are few glimpses of blue above, just hues of brown from beech, lime, sycamore, ash, birch, hornbeam, holly, elm, maple and oak enriched by a myriad palette of green.

I halt at a hollow and closing my eyes I can almost hear the rasping saw go back and forth and imagine the rising sawdust assailing my nostrils. I teeter on the edge of the old sawpit and visualise the two men, one at each end, working the long two-handled saw. One with his trilby slightly askew and the other, perhaps the underdog, in the base of the pit: the "daw" apprentice. Using the natural terrain of the woods they prepare lumber for further industry by bodger and furnituremaker.

I drift back to the present day but I am still wending my way further through bygone days. Unknowingly I pass a historic marling shaft entrance where lime and chalk were mined and later emerge into a clearing where once stood a bodger's hut.

This woodland world is so far removed from modern-day life it is as if I am travelling through a parallel universe. It is a land that truly belongs to nature and merely borrowed by man from time to time.

Chiltern Walks

Sarah-Jane Reeve

We walked up Coombe Hill and gazed
like gods or generals
across vale and plain
surveying our forgotten landscape, our terrain
ever present, yet eclipsed
by treeless civilization

We walked the springing step of half an hour
leading to the testing trudge of twenty miles
as the fields led us somewhere rare
to smell marigold and mallow
bejewelling the grasses
by steadfast standing stones

We walked back in time
along the Ridgeway like the ancients
unsheltered from the burning sun
washed by the rain
consulting the villagers
laden and hungry

We walked on chalk and flint
leaving the downs and climbing the hills
blowing our cobwebs away
remaking our neglected bond
with our uncared-for earth
searching for the upward path

The Chilterns On My Doorstep

Moyra Zaman

My footsteps regularly guide me to the Chess and Misbourne valleys which pass either side of where I live in Chesham Bois. The closest and most favoured valley is the Chess because of its tranquillity, the views and the variety that it offers. The Misbourne, nevertheless, has much to recommend it in its own way and because it comfortably links to the old town of Amersham.

The routes through the valleys meander along the length of their chalk river beds. The streams gurgle freshness as they trip on the flints and flow with slow deliberation down the years. Occasionally, the aquifer recedes when the weather is extremely dry and the river bed is exposed, but the situation is soon redressed when the groundwater levels return.

A circular walk in either valley can demand a steep climb, whether rising to Mop End from the Misbourne or to Latimer and Chenies from the Chess. Such is the nature of the Chilterns: rolling countryside, devoid of great mountains, but providing challenging inclines up its many hillsides. There is always a view to reward and inspire.

Each valley doffs its cap to a historic past. Set back on the hillside above the Misbourne, the splendid white stucco façade of Shardeloes, with its portico of Portland stone and Corinthian pillars, oversees the old town of Amersham. It was the ancestral home of the Drake family who presided over the town as Lords of the Manor and prospered between the sixteenth and eighteenth centuries. The virginal white exterior belies the fact that 5,000 babies entered the world through its womb during WW2 when it served as a maternity hospital for women from London. Now, converted into luxury flats, it is still a conspicuous and imposing landmark for walkers along the Misbourne valley and beyond.

The Chess boasts its own Manor in the form of Latimer House, identified by its convoluted red brickwork and tall Elizabethan-style chimneys. Historically, its origins stretch back to 1194 and it was fought over for many years until by 1615 it was bought by Lord William Cavendish and remained with his family for almost 350 years. The house as we see it today dates back to 1835 when it was rebuilt following serious damage by fire. Between 1847 and 1971 it became the home of the National Defence College and served as a top-secret Interrogation Centre for Military Intelligence during WW2. It's believed that Rudolf Hess was among the many prisoners who were lavishly housed and interrogated here. Latterly, after complete internal refurbishment, it has re-emerged as the De Vere Latimer Estate – a proud country hotel and conference centre. Guarded by the ancient yew tree in its grounds.

Below the house stands Latimer Park Farm (also a trout farm) which, from the first century, was the site of a Roman Farm Villa. On a quiet moment at the end of a winter's afternoon, when I've stood above it looking westward towards Chesham, I've noticed a solitary flag of smoke rising vertically from a hidden smokestack, and thought how reminiscent it was of those early settlements. In that silent moment it was an easy stretch of the imagination.

One is quickly drawn back to the present, however, by the plaintive cry of the beautiful Red Kites. These recent additions to the Chilterns have now become its signature bird. Having been introduced from Spain in the early

1990s by the RSPB and bred near Stokenchurch, they have now become synonymous with the region. They are mesmerising to watch as they circle with balletic grace. Their low manoeuvres allow us to appreciate their tawny glow as the sun strikes their bellies and with a flick of their fan tail, they turn and tease.

The kites oversee an area plentiful with wildlife. Besides the domestic cows, sheep and horses which graze the valleys at appropriate times and locations, foxes, badgers, and muntjac deer roam the region. In the streams themselves water voles and brown trout lurk, and kingfishers are spotted along their banks. In winter, skeletal trees expose the occasional cormorant, and herons, frozen like statues, try to avoid exposure.

In the shadow of Shardeloes, where the Misbourne bulges to a lake, water birds abound. In the winter, you cannot ignore the great cacophony of coots cutting the air discordantly, like a persistent child with a squeaky toy, or fail to notice the majestic flight of the Canada geese homing in on familiar ground. Meanwhile, the swans drift through their day with regal elegance. Come the spring, the mallards waddle on the grassy banks, encouraging their brood to the water's edge and leading their swim in convoy, like a school outing.

The Misbourne's flat-bottomed valley houses the Amersham cricket club in a contained scoop where the 'knock-on-wood' echoes down the years. A circuitous track avoids the clubhouse and leads to a narrow path before opening out between Shardoloes and the lake. Then an expansive vista draws you along its length towards the village of Little Missenden. Tall trees, hung with mistletoe clusters punctuate the route, while the evergreen woods on the brow of the hill keep a watchful eye on the grazing flocks below. Depending on the crop rotation, April can reveal the valley flanked in yellow flowering rape, its acid tones enhanced perhaps by thunderous indigo skies.

I hesitate to take you further on to Great Missenden itself; this was home to Roald Dahl for many years and still attracts his fans to his museum in the village. The countryside around provides the settings for his many tales and he would be saddened, as am I, to witness the devastation of the local ancient woods to carve a passage for the hotly debated HS2. Adding insult to injury, huge billboards covered with Hockney-like paintings of trees, have been erected to cordon off these areas of slain woodland.

We should be honouring the Chilterns' beechwoods which served their time providing raw materials for the bodgers to ply their trade. Those were the days when High Wycombe was rightly considered the chair-making capital of the world. As we stroll the woods south of the Chess today, we can still find the gouged-out basins where the trunks were hewn.

My love of the beechwoods is the lightness of touch that they bring, floating into existence, with bright green leaves fluttering on outstretched arms. At their feet the bluebells bide their time, until, in May, they spread their azure carpet on the woodland floor. A heady scent will greet you should you wander round the back of Latimer House and venture into Frith woods. This scene resonates throughout the valley's woodlands, spelling out the Chilterns at every turn.

The Chess valley flaunts its variety, trailing its route of twists and turns in undulating rhythms along its length. I often enter it by way of Blackwell Stubb Woods where crows circle noisily, claiming their perches high above in the tall trees. As I emerge on the path striding towards Blackwell Hall Farm, I follow a trail of sheep's wool suspended on barbed wire, like neatly placed bunting.

Then passing through the fields and rising up the steep incline strewn with flints, I slow my pace along the ridge to admire the valley below. In the foothills of Latimer I stop at the weir, a worthy water feature, then travel eastwards below Chenies. Soon I find myself in Frogmore Meadows Nature Reserve where an abundance of grasses, orchids and wildflowers flourish. Further still, the watercress beds appear, another remnant of a once thriving industry in the Chilterns. Lynchet terraces, extending back in time, crease the hillsides of Sarratt Bottom and linger as a historic reminder before the sound of the M25 kicks in.

Throughout the Chilterns, villages cower in splendour, paying homage to the vernacular. Names lure us back in time throwing up historic associations. And so it is in the vicinity of the Misbourne and the Chess with the likes of The Lee, Penn Street and Flaunden to name but a few.

As every season brings its charm and every footstep lodges us deeper into the landscape, hopefully we can all lay claim to a valley, a place where we can draw breath and feel renewed. I am happy to say that the Chess is unreservedly mine.

Lessons From Chiltern Wandering

Emma Barratt

This was not my birth place.
Soft hills, low rises, chalk vales adored by the spitfire red
kite,
the wooded banks and arched lanes to Tring,
that push up to chalky Ivinghoe Beacon, an old signal
point,
with wide skied, vivacious views where wild orchids tease
the eye
and the Duke of Burgundy descends.
Sky spread, drifting branches of beech promenade over
Ashridge
and guard the sky blest rides that gallop along the golden
valley
of a greying memorial to a Queen's reign.
There is mud to slip and slide on, ridges richly strewn with
mulch,
where the old Tudor monks haunt
and deer rut in these royal woodlands
and strut around, six-hundred-year-old oaks, as kings.
Waving winds ripple, stalk, skim over open reservoirs
where geese guard, mallards meander and swallows dive
roll.
Canals cut through the landscape where princely swans
traipse, on patrol,
along their smooth fluid course until winter numbs them,
trapping vivid coloured boats, belching grey smoke,
yet protecting the old heron's catch,
as the freckled silver-backed bream glide along the silted
bed.

Towering poplars border empty apple orchards,
with new nurseries forever filled with helleborine,
enchanter's nightshade
and fearful, foraging foxes.
Steep scrub hills are home to wandering sheep grazing on
calcareous grassland,
shaded by hawthorn as the larks soar and sing out their
caution.
Valleys drowned in endless soft rolling mists
disguise our great urban sprawl and secretly reveal it as
our own station,
a missing lost nation, a clandestine Camelot.
Lanes drift away from the roar of the tall daisy-fringed A41
and high streets hide histories which created our
constitution and built the palaces of democracy.
Villages shrink back from the flooding exuberant brooks
that meander through the
meadows where swimmers brave the intense situation.
Abandoned trenches, where soldiers trained, manoeuvre
over the ancient common,
to meet straight roman roads that marched legions to war.
Stately Chequers, a respite for the nation's leader, nestles
in slumbering security.
A zoo restrains a giant lion with a ferocious heart but
silent crown,
who glares down as gliders rise to Dunstable Down.
Wild planes and forests chase each other from Icknield
Way to Wendover and
memorials stand proud in churchyards, soaring above
trees or silently staring in
hushed squares.
A cathedral of air and glittering glades hide lovers who
whisper
amongst a rich, dark, white-chalked land that rolls to high
points

revealing the twinkling night time landscape of a folk-filled
vale dozing under a pole star.
A great pit, sunk to the core, now brims with brilliant,
mythical, blue blazing water.
Rugby pitches, football fields and cricket grounds blend
like patchwork, restrained
by wistful white blossom frosted Hawthorne hedges and
grazed by genuflecting daffodils.
When the hot, heavy, air fills with weighty pollen, farms
proudly
announce the bounteous rape seed meadows of gold,
streaked with pathways weaving to venerable pubs filled
with quenched satisfaction and elation.
So far from this island's stormy seas, gulls visit for the
peace that endures here,
in repose, a succulent green harbour graced by Summer's
soft sun,
decorated by Spring's blazing bluebell hum,
saved by Winter's wondrous white blanket of snow,
adorned by Autumn's stormy glow.
I raged for so long against this provincial place, a flawed
misfortune,
this mid-land where all is quiet and hush falls often.
So stealthily it seeped beneath my skin, deliberately lured
me in,
The people held me dear,
like a prayer, crushing my fear
and it all became my cloud nine,
this mid-land where all that was alien,
became a healing prescription to the ache of separation
a soothing life-giving, gentle consolation,
my final,
kindred,
destination.

CHAPTER 7

POTS AND PANS

Memorable Food From My Childhood

Lisbeth Cameron

Growing up in Denmark, I lived with my parents who were vegetarians. We never had meat at home, not that I missed it at all. Only on Christmas Eve did we have the traditional pork with crisp crackling on top together with all the trimmings, like browned potatoes, red cabbage, marinated marrow, and wonderful gravy. Browned potatoes are new potatoes lightly cooked in sugar in the pan. To the foreign mind it does not sound nice, until you try it. Unfortunately, when I left home in the sixties it was difficult when living in dormitories and training institutions to keep the vegetarian diet going so I lapsed.

If we went out to eat, which would only happen very rarely, we would then eat at a vegetarian restaurant. It was different but always very tasty. Since the restaurant was not too far away and we could buy vegetarian ingredients as well, we came home carrying heavy baskets with things like a special corn used for morning cereal called Kruska, and special soups and so on.

In Denmark in the summertime we would only have uncooked or raw food. Mother ingeniously carried out new ideas. We might have a cabbage leaf, filled with a row of grated carrots with a dressing of lemon, alongside rows of raisins, grated apple and grated raw potatoes. Have you ever tried to eat a raw potato? The taste is completely different from a cooked one. It was the only thing I absolutely disliked. But no doubt after having eaten the whole cabbage leaf with all the contents we could not eat any more. It was most filling.

My father was rarely seen in the kitchen, but he did like to make a special chocolate cake since it was not necessary to bake it. It consisted of lard and melted chocolate in between layers of biscuits. It had to be packed down well and put into the fridge. I have since improved the recipe by adding grated orange rind. I suppose that was too adventurous and too troublesome to use at the time.

Bloody Butter Beans

Richard Hounsfield

Curse them! I hate butter beans. I was nine years old and for over a third of my lifetime I had learned to detest these flaky horrors that got dumped onto my boring school dinner plate nearly every day. Joining in the nauseous array were soft diced carrots, double-scoops of mashed lumpy stodge and a dog-chew strip of leathery liver, all taunting me from a watery gravy puddle. What child-torturing lunatic decided this was a good idea?

Eww, urgh, the smell. Every few years I get a whiff of some so-called 'food' and it whisks me back to those dreaded school dinners, the grotesque images assaulting my unsuspecting senses for a queasy few seconds before being mentally ejected ASAP!

Six months ago, my partner served me yet another healthy meal, the sort I have spent most of my adult life 'accidentally' avoiding, and it was, er... delicious! Mmm, a chorizo stew with all sorts of goodness in it, green stuff, tomatoes and weird kidney-shaped cream-coloured fat flakes. Suzy gently ventured they were butter beans and I nearly spewed them across the table.

"Whaat?"

There they were staring up at me and I actually *liked* them. Half a century of hurt healed in an instant. Suzy laughed and I felt like a fraud caught in legal headlights. My lifelong rant against the grotesque butter bean suddenly felt like shallow childhood prejudice begat enduring empty falsehood.

Oh. Now I was exposed as unfairly denigrating this proteinous, low-fat, slow-release energy source that helps feed millions around the world, humble pie was being served as dessert.

Having been tasked to write about this bean I hate – sorry, love – I decided to look it up on Wiki. Unbelievable. This South American wonder is 'unmatched' in its ability to recruit defence when it needs it. When insect herbivores start voraciously munching on its leafy goodness (obviously having never suffered the school dinner disaster to put them off), this incredible plant releases chemical signals which attract predatory carnivores to munch on the greedy herbivores. So the butter bean gets Mafia-like protection and thus it survives. Bloody genius.

And do you know the Latin name for the eccentric butter bean? It is *Phaseolus lunatus*. Yes, LUNATUS! It's as mad as a box of frogs, explaining it as the main weapon of the child-torturing lunatic dinner lady.

Under Pressure

Kate Stanley

Growing up I had always been wary of pressure cookers, and with good reason as it turned out.

The Prestige pressure cooker was a fixture of my mother's kitchen, a faithful servant in the daily preparation of food. The potatoes and green vegetables for most evening meals were cooked in it to save time. (Microwave ovens were then the stuff of science fiction.) Cheaper cuts of meat would be tenderised, but always seemed a bit stringy to me. Carcases were rendered gelatinous to make stock, especially the poor old turkey after Christmas. The best thing that came out of the pressure cooker was the occasional steamed pudding, but I always detected a slight flavour of 'scrag end'.

Every evening the pressure cooker rattled away ominously on the stove top and the little air valve would be flipped down to bring it to pressure. It then hissed and squealed as if it were about to blow a gasket. There was initial relief when the kitchen timer pinged and the gas was turned off, but this was short-lived as the next stage was the most nerve wracking. The safest way to let the pressure reduce was to leave it to go down naturally until the meal was ready to serve. But oh no, my mother was both impatient and fearless: she would pick up the cooker and hold it under the cold tap to force it into submission. She would then flip the air valve up again, press firmly down on the weighted lid and twist to open it. It definitely knew who was boss. By this point I had usually left the kitchen.

Years later, some kind soul gave us a Prestige pressure

cooker as a wedding gift; I'm sure it wasn't on our list and I question their motivation. However, out of misplaced loyalty (and still in the absence of microwave ovens) just like my mother, I used it to reduce the cooking time of our meals. It seemed only sensible, if a little comical, to stand well back and flip the valve up or down at arm's length with a wooden spoon, and I don't think I ever subjected my pressure cooker to the cold water torture. It should have been nicer to me in return. I had more or less overcome my fear and become in my own eyes a domestic goddess. What could possibly go wrong? One Sunday afternoon a few months into married life, I was washing up after lunch. My husband had gone out to take his mother to a nursery to choose plants. There were no mobile phones.

I have no idea how it happened, although I suspect malicious intent from the 'Prestige'. While wiping off the fluffy residue of potatoes, my finger became well and truly stuck under the clamping mechanism of the lid. Bewildered and in pain, I didn't know what to do, other than panic. The only way to release my finger was to press down on the clamp and twist, something I just couldn't contemplate. I'm amazed I didn't faint, as I had once done at school after pricking my finger with an embroidery needle (I call it my Sleeping Beauty complex).

I would love to relate a dramatic, heroic ending to this sorry tale, but post-traumatic stress has blurred my memory. I know I went next door to ask for help, and I think pliers and a screwdriver were involved, but I would have had my eyes closed. I was released from my bondage before my husband arrived home. He could hardly believe what had happened and annoyingly thought it very funny. For many months I had a tingling sensation in that finger and couldn't bear to wear a ring, but I was thankful I'd been spared the indignity of turning up at A&E like the little boy with the saucepan or colander stuck on his head.

The pressure cooker lost its prestige status and was confined to the back of a cupboard, where it gave me the evil eye whenever I went rummaging for something. Funnily enough, it got lost when we moved house later that year.

The Kitchen Champ

Richard Hounsfield

Why do we all have them? Or maybe we don't. The items in the kitchen drawer that have come from Mum's or maybe even Grandma's. I'm not talking about precious heirlooms or sentimental ornaments but mundane kitchen implements.

I have a few of these loyal subjects, including Grandma's black Bakelite-handled tiny egg-spoons and a smuggled 'BCAL' engraved teaspoon from one of Dad's many flights. My favourite could even have been the ubiquitous 'Black Gnat' potato peeler. Yes, it really has a name. I didn't know that until just now, bashing around the utensils drawer. The Black Gnat as it shall forever now be called like some superhero potato-slayer, is something you'll all recognise immediately without giving it a second thought, simplicity being the hallmark of design brilliance and omnipresence the sign of success. It is about the same length as a fat marker pen with half of it being a tubular, black plastic handle, a plump cook's finger-width across. It always has tightly coiled red string winding half way along the handle (mine now a faded muddy orange after thirty years) that binds the metal peeling blade, complete with peeling slot and pointy end to gouge out the spud's eyes. The forever useful but boring potato peeler, yawn.

I'm still searching for my favourite, number one star: rattle, clatter... and there it is, unassuming, tucked away in the rear corner. 'The Champ' of them all, my most treasured non-valuable invaluable kitchen implement is the utterly faithful little whisk. It rests on my page as I write, dislodging the Black Gnat as the focus of my attention. It's more of a hero to me than any common-or-garden potato skinner.

Mum reckons she bought this whisk as a newly-wed in Chichester, which means it was probably made about three years before me, so we have been lifelong housemates. It is modest, only the length of my hand from the tip of the wooden handle to the apex of the egg-shaped oval of sturdy thick wire. The ends of the wire are twisted together to form a straight and strong wound shaft that disappears into the little cigar-size tatty wooden handle, a torpedo tapering away to a gently rounded end. This oval tenaciously holds a coil of unruly and springy-thin whisk-wire wrapped around it. It's not possible to get the little whisk out of the drawer and hold it for more than five seconds before you find yourself squashing the springy coil all the way around the oval, just to let it go with a satisfying 'ping' as it races back into egg-shape in a millisecond.

Only two-thirds of the red paint on the handle still clings to the wood. It is mottled, cracked, chipped and worn away completely in places with a barely-visible white line that once gave it a stylish chance. The letter 'H' of 'RICH' is all that remains of the marker pen ensuring my righteous claim to the little whisk when co-habiting with envious students with more important things to think about, until they realise they have no whisk of their own. Ha!

When it was bequeathed to me on leaving home, I would never have thought that this little anchor to my past, my kitchen comfort blanket, would have carried me through so many college hangover blues, whisking up the best comfort food ever. It's journeyed with me into adult life creating happy memories of treating my later kids to the guilty pleasure of Angel Delight mousse.

I guess when I was about seven and deemed mature

enough to be in charge of making a proper mess, I whisked my first Angel Delight mousse with this masterpiece of kitchen understatement. Aged 57, I whisked about my thousandth 'AD' just last week. In the days before the whisk lost its shine Mum defended our teeth by making sure that Angel Delight was a tasty diversion from the sweet shop. So all flavours were thoroughly road-tested, the discontinued, sickly-sweet, pastel-coloured peach flavour being the one I miss most today.

Of course, to create the world's best Angel Delight, you also need the ideal non-identical kitchen twin for your whisk, and that is the perfectly-sized battered old Tupperware mixing bowl that sits close by in the cupboard, seemingly unnoticed but never forgotten. This kitchen 'twin-set' has ruled at the epicentre of Angel Delight culinary excellence for as long as Muhammed Ali's name has been remembered. The little whisk and his bowl-mate have beaten off all whisk-comers like the true Champ.

Apart from the occasional scrambled egg after I left home for college, the dependable whisk has rarely seen outings for more exotic foods, partly because there is no more exotically-named food than 'Angel Delight' but mostly because I don't know what else to whisk. However, I took ridiculous pride in handing down the little-whisk-and-battered-bowl technique for the perfect AD to my offspring. But I'm afraid they went over to the Dark Side, forever corrupting the Angel Delight with hand-held electric blenders.

If you believe in 'panpsychism', then this little whisk would have a consciousness of its own. I hope it would be proud to celebrate its sixtieth birthday and as a wise sexagenarian reflect on how well he has served his loyal and cherishing owner, rather than fume at being left in a dark and cluttered utensil drawer for six decades and bashed around almost every day whilst some ignorant human decided a stupid spatula or even the loathsome and sneering Black Gnat was more useful, again.

And for those that want to see the loyal subjects...

KITCHEN DRAWER HEROES!

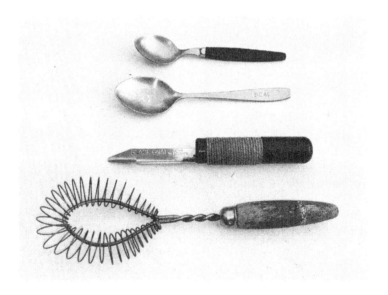

CHAPTER 8

LIFE

You Used To Be Funny
(An Ode To Parenting)

Richard Hounsfield

Dedicated to the children who may one day understand.

This fractious stream of consciousness came about because I was after some kitesurfing advice from a long-lost work colleague, last known about twenty years ago. Discovering that he now lives in New York, my tentative email was sent, including the question:

"Do you have family or are you still living it up as a bachelor?"

Seb wrote a great re-connection reply about kitesurfing and included this:

"I'm married with a three-year-old and another on the way. We just bought a house in the 'burbs about 30 minutes outside of the city."

Wow, such news, the free-spirited dreadlocked surf dude has settled down. My first reaction? 'You've no idea what's coming, my friend!' I was sitting on the sunny overground Metropolitan Line train rattling from Baker Street to Chesham, tapping away on the keyboard. Seb had unintentionally poked the tiger, unleashing frustrations about growing kids that I'd been subconsciously tossing around for a while. An hour sped past as, chuckling away, I retched up the following cathartic download on parenting teenagers...

***

Hi Seb,

Great to hear from you and congrats on having gained a wife, a young child and one brewing. My instinctive advice is to enjoy the first thirteen years while you are their undisputed hero before one day, without really noticing, you will have turned into a total embarrassment of a parent who is not even allowed to drop them at the school gates anymore. As they start shedding dependence for independence over the next few years, be ready because what authority you thought you had will be tested to destruction and your ego will shrink to an atomic dot.

Strap in for at least seven years of monosyllabic, entitled behaviour where you know nothing and are forced to listen to the moronic logic of a teenage force of nature that has not connected with their frontal cortex yet who will tell you exactly how the world works, drawing on their vast experience of at least nought years as a fully-fledged adult which is clearly a far more informed position than your decades dealing with the very issues they are in the process of f*cking right up.

As a loving parent, you will of course bear all these effronteries with stout resolve and not succumb to sobbing every night, mourning the passing of the beautiful sweet happy wonderful child that once adored you but now seems solely to exist to suck the lifeblood from your brittle veins and drain your wallet, which is the price you have to pay for these tortured 'privileges'. And when all is said and done, although they have literally taken you to the edge of madness, you love them every inch of the way. After all, it's your fault they are here in the first place and they are half you anyway so how can you not love them?

All those years of nurturing, trying to casually gift your wisdom, teaching by example or just ramming home without patience, some core values of love, respect, integrity, tolerance and compassion, appear to have been wasted. Any traces of these slow-blossoming traits are rapidly incinerated in the emotional equivalent of an eighteen-year-old exploding supernova. Don't even think about applying any of your granite-strong reasoning to another emerging crisis because the dismissive Kryptonite demolition by smug teenage illogic will shrivel it to a wayside footnote, only to hawkishly gust up on the wind with an exasperated 'I told you so' whoosh, after the predictable chaos ensues.

The metamorphosis hibernation has begun, and you will only learn sometime hence whether your sage values had ever properly seeded; so even though you didn't manage to live by them with perfect poise, your impatient and vicarious hope lives on.

I have been reliably told, by my mother of course, that eventually the scowling locust that lurks either upstairs in the dark or downstairs with one elephantine arm hoovering the fridge while refusing to acknowledge your interfering presence, will emerge as a person that does not think only of themselves, but starts to open their eyes to the sensitivities of others and actually becomes pleasant and rewarding and funny to be around. You used to be funny but unfortunately all humour has evaporated from your battered brain in the last few years and now your paradoxically parasitic 'I-don't-need-you!' offspring are the reasonable, funny and likeable beings that you used to be.

When you return home from slavishly earning the crust that you pour into your unappreciative teenage money pit, you wearily pause at the protective front door, bracing your mind and body for tonight's dinner-table assault; will it be a rare glimpse of harmony and smiles or the familiar feeling of falling into a casserole of nonsense? You try to engage your troubled teens and counsel them through the age of anxiety, battling to duck the 'cancel culture' spew aimed squarely at you by the growling teen-dog. But when the barking subsides and the green shoots of maturity peek through, enlightening moments flash up as you listen and learn; as new insight gets handed back up a generation and they teach you things you should now know: the world changes one person at a time; what you used to say may no longer be okay. So having your worn-out eyes widened can be a gift from your young, as you help each other on your diverging journeys. These are the trillion moments of cognitive history where wisdom and experience synergise with the energy and smarts of youth, banging the cultural clock forward another notch.

So if you didn't cock it up completely, there is a chance they are worth knowing, and they will remember that once upon a time you were a genuine hero, and will befriend you in a way that is unique and trust you like they can no other. Hopefully they will honour you into your senior years and if you are lucky enough to have the experience repeat itself without responsibility, otherwise known as 'grandparenting', you will eventually be honoured, when their own thirteen years on the parent hero-pedestal have passed, with the dubious privilege of listening to your children's wailing lament, "What happened to my beautiful sweet happy wonderful child?" and wonder if they will ever give you the credit you deserve for a life in their service.

But you don't need it anyway because you love them unconditionally. This, my friend, is the irrefutable and irresistible circle of life.

Let me know how you get on.

Cheers, Rich

***

I never sent this reply to Seb. What on earth would he have made of it as a new father if this is what he had to look forward to? Perhaps my experience of ten years of teenager wars blasting me through middle age into the leftover of just wanting my own life back is not going to be Seb's journey.

But I always felt I should at least send it to him before it went anywhere else, so if you're reading this, he will now have it – along with my heartfelt best wishes for the tough part of the parenting journey, for which he has unwittingly signed up.

One ideally hopes to enter the 'teenage years' as a parent with child, riding them out until hopefully, you emerge as a parent and friend. And if you're really resilient you'll still have your sense of humour because remember, you used to be funny.

The River

Sarah-Jane Reeve

We had just moved to a small village in Surrey and I often went out exploring on my bike. It was Boxing Day afternoon, and I felt the urge to do just that. I had finished my book, and suddenly felt I had had enough of TV, my sisters fighting over dolls, and the stuffy indoors.

I grabbed my jacket and wellies and slipped out of the side door. The cold air instantly wiped away my sluggishness as I wheeled out my bike from the sideway. I pedalled down the snow-silenced street to the field at the end, iciness biting my ears. Exhilarated by the white beauty of the field under a foot of snow, I threw down my bike, impulsively turned to my left, and saw the stream in the distance. I struggled through a gap in a barbed wire fence, and staggered down a slope. There it was.

It was shallow and frozen at the edges, the ice cracked in places like broken glass. The stream flowed to my left past the backs of the houses. It was stony and clear and only a couple of inches deep at this end. I started to wade in the water, enchanted by the way that the snow dusted trees on both banks formed an arch of branches across the stream. It was completely quiet: as it was Christmas even the main road traffic behind the trees was silenced. No one was about. No one knew I was there. A little watery sunlight forced its way through the grey cloudy sky. I found myself wading in the direction of my house, wondering if it was possible to go past it to the entrance to our street. I took the chance of a small adventure.

As I waded upstream of course, the river got deeper, for

it was a river now in my imagination. This was probably what explorers coped with all the time, I thought. Then it occurred to me that if the water went over the top of my wellies and soaked my jeans then that would be the end of the expedition. I was vaguely aware that if my parents found out I was doing this they would not be happy and I would probably be banned from doing it again.

I kept on wading, causing small ripples and splashes that disturbed the silence. I slipped on a stone and grabbed a branch to keep myself steady but luckily the water did not go into my boots. The action disturbed a shower of snowflakes which floated down into the river. I spotted a rubber ball bobbing along, probably the result of a missed shot at goal in Kevin Frances's back garden over to my left. I was going to leave it there – it served him right for calling me `beanpole' because of my skinny legs.

After ten minutes, I looked around and realised that I was behind my house but I was standing about four feet below the fence at the top of the bank. I held on to another branch and hauled myself up. I clung on to a concrete post, then the top of the fence and found a knothole in the feathered planks that I could peep through. I had to hang on tightly; one slip and I would have to explain wet clothes.

I looked across the garden to the lighted kitchen window. My parents were standing in the kitchen talking. I had the delicious feeling of being able to see them while they could not see me. I realised I had become invisible. They wouldn't even guess I was there. My mother was making tea and putting out mince pies on a plate. My grandmother who was visiting for Christmas, was ironing a tablecloth. They were in the world of home. It looked trivial, safe and predictable. I was outside, adventurous, independent. This was rather satisfying: I wasn't just an explorer, I thought, I could also be a spy.

I came out of my reverie as I realised that darkness was creeping around me and it was getting colder. I was still clinging to the fence with frozen fingers. I couldn't see a way out to the entrance to our street; the river seemed to flow into a culvert beside the main road. I started to climb down the bank but suddenly I slid on mud, scraped my knee on a stone sticking out of the bank, and splashed into the water. I winced and finally one boot filled up with icy water. I gasped in shock, and wobbling on the other foot struggled to empty the welly and put it back on. Still, I was relieved that I was not completely drenched. If they asked, I would say I fell off my bike.

Now I was hungry and shivering. Afternoon tea would be on the table soon and they would start calling me. I waded back the way I came, as the melting snow slid off the branches into the stream.

A Grey Cashmere Jumper

Emma Barratt

Once it was, for my dad, a woollen prize,
a beautiful soft silky, grey, cashmere jumper,
a gift from the Gobi Desert in a large man size.
He wore it often, a gentle haven, while carrying the new
baby daughter he adored.
A mellow surface for my beloved face when I was tucked
up in his embrace.
I snuffled into it wistfully while sleeping and dampened it
lightly when weeping.
When I was nearly one year old, it shrank in a hot wash.
So, my dad stored it in the airing cupboard, lonely,
ignored where it languished.
When I was a little older and my baby voice was much
bolder,
I was noisily discontented in my cot and could not rest
yet needed to be left to avoid my parents becoming
grouchy dinosaurs and depressed.
My parents despaired as they listened, suddenly an idea
occurred to my dad
how sadness might be conquered.
He took the tiny soft grey jumper and laid it by my head.
I perceived the kindness and even, a smell, so familiar.
Quick as a flash, I grabbed a fistful, pulled it to my chest,
waving my little legs with happiness and zest.
My tears melted as I drifted to dreamland, carefree by
cashmere command.
Eventually from my cot to a bed I travelled with my
comforting cloak of magical certitude.

The jumper journeyed everywhere I went, like a guardian angel wisely sent.

One day my daughter, almost ten, whose attitude normally resembled a fine state of zen,

planned an adventure with school to stay in a tent, that she thought was really cool.

Just as she was leaving, sadness overwhelmed her, so inspired by my Dad

I courageously gave my daughter, my shrunken cashmere protector.

I handed it from my hands to hers, then she held it to her face and smiled.

How simple, strange and farsighted, what comfort it can bring,

a slip of clothing, carefully bequeathed.

Lockdown Moments

Moyra Zaman

(Written in May 2020 about the first lockdown)

Languishing in bed with cup of tea
and books at hand; rising only
as needs must or tummy rumbles
to a brunch the day half gone.

Virtual meetings zoom into my,
otherwise, unpunctuated life;
phone calls, emails, texts and
YouTube 'smilers' occupy the days.

One hearty laugh a day will, surely,
exercise my lungs and, holding still
between my breaths, I count to ten
and reassure myself I'm well.

Escaping from the belching bulletin
of news and COVID updates,
I seek a sunny, silent spot to write
and gainfully compose my thoughts.

Sandwiched between the lawnmower
and the barking dog –
I'm quietly reassured
my neighbours still exist.

My husband, sticking closely to advice
to stay at home, exercises round me
and our meagre plot – an hour of
daily circuits wearing out the lawn.

The road is chalked for Sunday's sponsored fun,
saving the gorillas – a forty-two-mile walk
imagined on the Yorkshire moors,
where it would have run.

Indoors, I benefit from yoga on the mat;
then every other day, my Nordic
Walking poles direct me to the park,
muzzled and minding my two-metre distance.

Essential only trips to Tesco,
cautiously approached; spacing
and queueing, in the over-seventies slot –
pasta and toilet rolls, high up on the list.

A Thursday evening catch-up with the neighbours,
clapping for the front-line and NHS;
kitchen pans unite and fireworks shout
appreciation – stories are exchanged.

A masked plumber visits one door down
allowing the ritual washing of the hands;
a cautious lady microwaves her mail, oblivious
of the bank card tucked within.

Redundant cars won't start – a recharge remedy?
No way! New battery required.
I toss the keys and RAC's quick service brings a smile
my Focus, with a dirty grin, pleads, 'Drive me please!'

Wham, bang – catastrophe! The folk, two down, break
sweat!
One wall down, a garage door hollering in pain.
Foot slips bizarrely and the car's a write-off, towed away
before the driver comprehends his shock.

It's seven o'clock when I realised my watch
had stopped two hours ago; the days,
already befuddled, become a timeless existence,
paying homage only to the sun.

Summer's poked her nose in early, sniffing out
exotic curries and the BBQs.
Guitars harmonise the broken conversations, competing
with the children's splashing screams.

And yet, hot tempers rise in crowded tenements,
where weary walls have captured space and
sleep cannot assuage the bellies' hungry claw;
masked moments in the park – the only brief relief.

Most parents in perpetual motion,
juggling pressures of home-schooling;
deadlines still at work for some, others furloughed,
and concerned – counting costs.

I hear of friends in care homes,
worried and confused; a cousin's hit by COVID –
a nurse of course – recovered, back on duty,
overworked and short of PPE.

The pressure's on for tests, requests
for vaccines being researched, misleading
use of disinfectants advocated for injection –
Trump's frightful flippancy and ignorance exposed.

Meanwhile, myriad options stream my way
encouraging productivity: learn a language,
join Jo Wicks, view free films – filling time like
gluing cracks, lest we should fall apart.

Yet, cracks are our salvation now – space to breathe,
consider and reflect – oozing out compassion,
new ideas and creativity, to face the new world order,
when this lockdown's done.

Don't Forget Us

Sarah-Jane Reeve

While I was visiting my sister one day she said she wanted to show me something she had found.

It was an old photograph album belonging to my grandmother, Florence, found in a box of my father's papers. It was full of photos of my grandmother, her relatives, her husband, and her son, my father. The small prints were taken between the 1920s and the 1940s, and my sister and I spent an enjoyable evening poring over them trying to figure out who was who. Photography had provided a window into the past.

But the best photo had been taken over a hundred years ago, and had been printed larger than the others. It is of a family group, the Jackson family: Ada, the mother (my great-grandmother), and her three children: Florence (my paternal grandmother), Fred, Violet and their dog. Ada is sitting on a chair in the middle of the photo, and the children are standing around her, and the family dog is sitting in the bottom right-hand corner.

My grandmother, Florence, looks about 10 years old in this picture. As she was born in 1908, and going by the clothes, I estimate the photo was taken towards the end of the First World War. Florence is wearing a white smock-like dress and although she is pretty she has slightly protruding front teeth and a shy look. Her long hair is pinned to one side and curled into ringlets, presumably for the occasion, and so is the hair of her younger sister Violet. She stands in front of Florence, looks about 6 years old and still has a babyish roundness to her face. She also wears white, a similar dress to Florence's but shorter, with knee-length lace-trimmed white shorts visible below the hem. She also wears smart, white, calf-height boots tied with ribbons. Violet holds her mother's hand.

To the other side of Ada is Fred. He looks about 9. He stands on the right, opposite Florence. He is dressed in a crumpled school blazer and tie and the dog sits in front of him. I get the impression that his hair has been combed to one side for him. He is the only one to attempt a smile – he has a cheeky grin, a smirk. It is possible that smiling is not the fashion for formal family photographs, but Fred can't resist.

The dog wears a collar and is sitting to attention and looking straight at the camera, or the photographer. He or she is definitely one of the family.

But the centre of the photograph is Ada, sitting on a chair. She is wearing a white blouse and a long, dark skirt made of practical, hardwearing material, and her hair is pinned up. She can only be in her thirties but has an almost stern, careworn expression on her oval face, with her mouth turning down slightly on the right side. I can tell she is the one keeping it all together: she looks like an army wife; her husband William was a sergeant major. She and Violet have the same deep-set eyes, and Florence has her oval face. But not only is Ada not giving us a smile, I get the impression that for her this photograph business is just something she is required to do.

So, everyone is turned out in their Sunday best, but where are they? I can tell this is not a studio shot. At the back I can see a fence, with a glimpse of a leafy bush on the left, and what looks like the top of a dustbin lid to the right. I would guess they are outside in the back yard.

Did they really persuade a professional photographer to come down to their back yard with a tripod and a black cloth to put over the camera? It seems unlikely. This could be an early snapshot. A little research tells me that during the First World War, portable cameras were mass produced. Kodak sold thousands of what they called 'Vest Pocket' cameras. These small cameras were popular with soldiers wanting family snaps to carry with them. Another family camera sold from 1900 was the 'Box Brownie', I remember my grandad Leonard, Florence's husband, showing me his battered 'Brownie' when I was a child.

As my great-grandfather William is not in the picture I fondly assume that he is taking the photograph, unless a friend is taking it for him. Perhaps he was away, or going away on duty, and wanted a photo of his family. If this was the First World War, they must have been worried that they might not see him again. Perhaps that is the reason for my grandmother's serious look.

What happened to the Jacksons? My sister, our mother and I searched our memories for conversations with relatives over the years: fortunately, William survived the war, eventually gave up the army and became a security guard. He and Ada lived well into their eighties in South London and died in the mid-1960s.

But they had their tragedies. They lost poor Violet early; she died at the age of 14 in a tuberculosis hospital. Fred died in his forties of cancer sometime in the 1950s.

I remember Florence, my grandma, really well, as she was a big part of my childhood. She cut her hair short in the 1920s, and always loved dancing, parties and clothes; I remember dressing up in her old satin evening dresses as a child. She worked as a telephonist in London when telephones were rolled out to the masses. Then she travelled all over the world with her husband Leonard, a surveyor with the Imperial Air Ministry before, and during, the Second World War. She lived until her mid-eighties and died in 1993.

I have a copy of the lost photograph on my desk at home and I look closely at their faces from time to time, but there is no hint of their fates in their expressions. They gaze at me across time from their backyard, frozen in that moment. I'm so glad we found them. And if there is a message, I think they say to me what they said to William: We are your family. This is what we look like. Don't forget us.

The Linen Cupboard

Emma Barratt

The cupboard background was painted a heavenly soft sky blue. It was a pretty piece of furniture yet it was slightly out of place in the austere manor house that was otherwise filled with the dark oak furniture which the family had acquired centuries before.

The cupboard was in one of the eight spare bedrooms, this one was at the back of the house. The room had large windows which allowed the sunlight to penetrate and delicately fade the paintwork on the cupboard. It seemed to Elke that the cupboard must have been a woman's choice, as the front was decorated with garlands of tulips and leaves. The edges were painted a warm, pinkish red. White lilies and roses danced across the doors and up the sides. The garden had been brought into the room. Elke gazed upon it for a while, appreciating its beauty.

The top half of the cupboard was made up of two, large, prettily decorated doors. Under the upper cupboard were three long drawers. All were locked. Elke took a key from her cardigan pocket and examined it for a while before tentatively trying it in the lock of one of the doors. She breathed a sigh of relief as the cupboard door swung wide open.

She took a step back to look at what she had discovered. There were three long, deep, widely spread shelves that went the entire length of the cupboard. Each shelf was weighed down with soft white linens of various sorts. Bed sheets, tablecloths, nightwear, were all beautifully pressed and tied with narrow blue silk ribbons.

The drawers beneath were filled to overflowing with white lace-trimmed handkerchiefs, shirts and other old undergarments. The tiny lace lavender bags that were perched on top of each of the piles and pushed into the corners of the drawers were still faintly fragrant. The cupboard had remained locked for years until she had finally found the key at the bottom of one of her mother's old wooden jewellery boxes a week ago.

It was not until she had emptied the jewellery box entirely that she noticed the velvet lining was coming away from the bottom and tucked underneath was the dull brass key with a length of blue silk ribbon attached. She had held the key in her hand while examining it and had guessed it was the cupboard key because of the blue silk ribbon which exactly matched the blue paint on the cupboard. The illusive lost key was finally discovered. Nobody had been able to open the cupboard for forty years. A few had suggested just using a crowbar to pry it open, but no one had wanted to risk damaging its delicate paintwork.

Elke stood and looked at the mountain of white. It was perfect, so tidy and elegant. She reached out a hand and placed it upon the sheets in front of her. She stroked the soft cool cotton, felt its gentleness under her hand. She lifted one sheet to her face and inhaled. There was a slight musty tang underneath the faint traces of lavender. It would all need to be cleaned and sorted before it could be put to use or given away.

She placed that first sheet she had taken out of the cupboard on the old wooden framed double bed behind her. Elke could only remember the room being used once and that was by her grandfather during a visit nearly thirty years ago, just before he had died. He had always seemed a sour, surly and sad figure to her.

Elke turned and reached into the cupboard, tipping her

whole body forward so she could reach the sheets at the back of the first shelf. She lifted the sheets out and staggered towards the bed with the pile. She returned again to the cupboard and lifted out the next pile. As she did so, an old envelope fluttered to the floor. She looked down at it while still holding the sheets in her arms. She bent down and peered at the spiky black scrawl across the envelope. She stood straight for a moment to try and remember, was the handwriting familiar? She placed the sheets on the bed and turned again to look at the letter. She stood over it, wondering for a moment until she bent down gingerly to pick it up, noticing the twinge of pain in her knee as she did so.

She held the letter, felt its weight, turned it over and over and then smoothed its surface. She decided to finish her task, the letter should wait, so she placed it on the window sill by the cupboard and returned to lifting out the sheets. Eventually she had emptied all but the top shelf but to do this she had to pull the edge of the sheets, bracing her feet a little to ease them off. As the sheets began to slip and fall into her arms, she stumbled a little. As she recovered, she noticed another letter had fallen onto the floor. She added the armful of sheets to the mountain gathering on the bed, turned and bent down and picked up the next letter and placed it carefully next to the other letter on the window sill. The cupboard was finally empty but she was curious and so stood on her tiptoes to try to see if there was anything lurking on the top shelf. As she couldn't quite see, she left the room, walking down the narrow, wooden-floored corridor to her book-lined study to get the intricately carved wooden step ladder.

Elke warily climbed the little ladder and finally got a clear view to the back of the shelf. Another letter lay resting there, slightly crumpled, as if it had been pushed to the back in a hurry. She leaned in and ran her hand across the back of the cupboard, trying to feel if anything else might be lodged there. The roughness of the inside of the cupboard made her withdraw her hand quickly; a small abrasion was left on the palm of her hand. She grabbed the letter and again examined the handwriting. It was the same as the previous two letters.

She climbed gingerly down the step, turned and placed the final letter by the others. Pausing for a moment she gazed out of the window at the abandoned garden beyond, its return to wilderness giving new life to the old oak, its canopy full and green, now strangely rejuvenated. She could see the white roses had grown tall and straggly, the honeysuckle sprawled amongst the brambles, the ivy creeping across the paths. The butterflies danced lightly over the escaping lavender.

She picked up the letters and peered a little closer to see if she could work out who they were addressed to. She thought she recognised the name but her memory was too vague to be sure. It seemed from the envelope that they were not addressed to any of her family.

The three envelopes were all white and of a good quality. Each had been opened with a letter knife across the top. The post mark was too faint on the first envelope to work out where it might have come from and there was no stamp left. The second envelope still had on it an old soft green stamp that was obviously American; she could just make out 'In God we Trust' written above a tiny Statue of Liberty. On the third envelope there was a barely decipherable New York post mark and another soft green American stamp.

She wondered how these letters from so far away, addressed to someone she could not recall, had ended up in the linen cupboard.

Elke was uncertain about reading the letters; it felt as if

she was invading someone's privacy. She stood for a while, staring at them, then, suddenly, she took first letter out of its envelope and began to read. It took time, as the handwriting was a spiky, hastily written scrawl. There was only one page of white paper, it was thick and when she held it up to the light, she could see a watermark. There was no address, date or name on the page. Just an endearment.

January, 28th 1946

My dearest

How calmly the days go now. Each morning I rise and watch the birds in the tiny garden as they flutter round the apple tree as it changes from blossom to unfurling leaf and small green fruit.

My room is airy, full of light. I am always warm, even when the snow falls and the streets here are buried under icy, huge drifts.

I hear the sounds of the other tenants around me and I am reassured at this evidence of life.

I remember each day that you hid me, locked inside, silent, seeing only the light of day from the inside of that great cupboard. The constant darkness when I could only hear the day happening, your light movements, the cries of your children, the voice of your mother as she reprimanded them. Every day I would try to work out what you were all doing. I would pray. How I loved the early afternoons when they rested and you played for me, the soft sounds of Chopin upon the air, drifting to my confined, blacked-out world. I could imagine your hands, your fingers brushing over the keys. Your playing would take me to the cool woods and flowing river of my childhood. Beethoven would cry out, I could hear your distress, your heart beating as you played.

Yesterday I smelt lavender and thought of you, the linen, my cupboarded world.

Dearest how you held me in the soft light of early morning as you helped me from my sanctuary. Your whispering endearments soothed me. How my arms and limbs ached from lying so still for so long. You wanted to ease the pain but how my muscles screamed at the effort of trying to walk. I was so afraid that I would never be able to escape if I needed to. How much more delectable was my food, the bread, water, a sweet apple, just because you had brought it to me! Your favourite poems soothed me. I did escape, not from you, but because of you, to safety my love.

You saved my life.

I know you are alone, but I am here, waiting for you. Waiting for you to give up your life. I know how much I ask of you.

You kept me alive, kyrie, alive.

I will return, rescue you, give you a life.

With my love, dearest,

Gavriel

Elke put the letter down on the window sill and calmly took out the next letter. It was dated January 2nd 1947 and was a mere eight lines long.

January 2nd 1947

Dearest

I have no money, but I will return. You will see me again. Be patient, for me. I will find us a way. I have found work and I save a little each day. Put your fear aside my love, to do otherwise will only blight your days. The job has prospects and the university has agreed to let me sit exams to requalify here. It will not be long; we can survive the many days.

Do not give up hope for us. I am saving all that I can so I can bring you to me. We will be together. Every day we get a little closer to what we both desire.

Take care of yourself, be kind, be patient. We will both be free.

Your beloved and one love,

Gavriel xxx

She took out the final letter and from its worn appearance Elke could tell it had been read over and over again. The letter looked as if it had been crumpled up and then straightened out again. This time there was an address.

Apartment 2
59th and west
New York
October 15th 1948

Dearest

I enclose the money for your boat trip. You will need only a warm coat and a small casc to bring your belongings. The boat will depart on December the fifth. Bring only what you need for the journey, nothing more. Leave behind all but your memories. If you bring anything of value, they can accuse you of theft and set the authorities after you. I know how hard this will be. You must be so very careful if we are not to be discovered. Bring only what they will not miss. We must not be traced, we cannot be found, my love, to all intents and purposes we must be lost.

Jakiel will meet you at Café Salut by the entrance to the port, with your passport and papers. He will find you; I have described you well. You must leave under dark, remember you must tell no one, no one! Never forget they will try to find you. I am so fearful that we will lose this chance and our happiness depends on it.

The boat will be crowded but talk little, stay unnoticed. Only once you have landed here and through customs will you be completely safe. I understand how lonely you have been but it is only for a little longer.

I know that leaving will be hard, I know how much you will be giving up. Survival requires a terrible sacrifice for you my love. Never forget, I love you. I will always love you.

We will make a life together; we will be free!

In time your children will visit, they are nearly grown, they will understand. Bless them with love's words, remind them you will be forever in their hearts but tell them nothing. It is not goodbye.

We will be together.

Your beloved,

Gavriel xxxx

She put the last letter back down on the window sill with the others. She took deep soothing breaths. She could not believe what she had unearthed, now at this moment, when the house was to be sold, when everything was over. She turned and stared at the cupboard. She realised it was indeed deep enough and it would be possible to hide a person inside it. How long he must have been hidden for and suffer was hard to imagine. She glanced at the key in the lock. It must have been so frightening and exhausting for them both.

Could her mother still be alive after all this time? Was she with him? Since the day her mother disappeared, no one had any idea what had happened, whether she was alive or not. All Elke remembered was that when she last saw her, she bent to kiss her goodnight, smoothed her bed sheet, stroked her forehead with her thumb and sung her a gentle lullaby as she drifted off to sleep. She remembered her enormous love for her and how it had never dimmed. Grief stood starkly in her heart, all her family had been wounded, stained forever. The loss had been horrendous, they had eventually assumed she might have died, yet they had never been able to grieve.

Elke slowly sat down on the bed and began to weep. The grief was overwhelming but slowly her sobs began to subside. Joy and warmth began to seep through her as she realised, she might see her mother again. Her mother was in America. Her mother was forever found.

Summer It Is

Lisbeth Cameron

My brother in Denmark invited me to his summer barbecue. He only does it every second year – so I wanted to go. It normally involves 27 people from the family including 12 children of all ages. Everyone would come – crossing the country in cars, trains, ferries, and buses from all directions.

For me it involved trains, a plane, and more trains. In the airport I had to let go of my lovely hand cream, which was more than the required 100ml. This was only because in the recent past a fanatic, irresponsible, deranged individual wanted to kill other people. Now we all have to suffer the consequences.

On arrival, even though I am Danish I was not sure I was on the right platform. I asked the nearest woman who turned out to be English. I can manage that language too, but she was not sure about the train either. At the bottom of the stairs, I asked an approaching man. He was Spanish and thought I wanted help with the suitcase. I managed to thank him, but I was still not sure about the train.

A train approached; inside I asked two women, they turned out to be French – all I could say was "Merci", but it was the right train. In spite of it being tourist season I still find it incredible when I come home to my small, first country, that one needs to converse in several languages just to find the right platform. At the end of the journey I was collected by my brother and taken the 12 kilometres to his garden and lovely summerhouse.

I had been travelling from 9 a.m. to 7 p.m. Half the family had arrived, and we all sat down outside to a wonderful meal until the sun set. The house could not accommodate all the family so five tents of different sizes were erected on the lawn for us.

The next morning several of us started with a cool, refreshing swim in the fjord. After breakfast with baked morning buns, some of us followed my brother on a walk into the nearby forest. As always, he was carrying a pocket dram of bitter snaps (aquavit) which we shared while we listened to his knowledge of forestry and history.

The days passed with playing with the children, chatting to people not seen for a long time, meeting newly married partners, admiring babies and catching up on events. Charlie who was born with one half leg, and was now an adult, entertained the children by demonstrating what he could do with his three toes on a foot that came out from his right knee.

My cousin called for a competition in which all the children tried to eat as many cream buns as possible within three minutes. There was cream everywhere, not only from ear to mouth, but hands and arms were covered as well. Some had to stop halfway, but the oldest boy won by consuming seven buns. He got a diploma printed with his name on to prove it.

In order to cope with so many people my sister-in-law had organised us by putting up a rota in the kitchen. It listed all the jobs which had to be done: laying the table, peeling potatoes, entertaining children, changing nappies on children and anyone else who needed it, taking the official photographs, and it included a person who would watch over sobriety and be ready to drive people to the doctor. Some signed up, but remarkably we discovered the Queen and other famous names had offered their services as well.

My husband when collecting me at Gatwick could immediately see I was refreshed, relaxed, and renewed, by saltwater, sunshine, and laughter. My sister-in-law sent a letter saying that when all was quiet again and she was scrubbing the kitchen floor, which was really dirty, she enjoyed doing it, remembering what a lovely time we all had, without any quarrels and how everyone had chipped in, helping, and taking care of each other. She might even do it again next year and not wait for another two years.

The Shopping Trip

Sarah-Jane Reeve

One December in the mid-1990s I felt restless, not at all Christmassy and in need of a small adventure, so I joined a walking tour of Turkey. We started by flying into snowy Istanbul.

The first day we were free to explore the city as we wished. So after the trip to the Blue Mosque and a boat ride on the Bosphorus, some girls and I decided to visit the Grand Bazaar. It was an international tour and our little team consisted of Julia, who owned a mailing and packaging business in Texas; Clare, a nurse from Ireland; Sally, originally from France, a retired school teacher from Surrey, and myself.

We found ourselves standing at the huge doors of the Grand Bazaar, keen to get out of the ice and snow. I was glad to be enveloped by warm air, sweet with sugar and spices, and the loud hum of hundreds of people busy with shopping and selling. In front of us were several pathways bordered by little shops. There were also stalls that were covered with a confusion of brightly coloured goods that were piled high, festooned from hooks and displayed in tottering pyramids from floor to ceiling. We were overwhelmed – where should we start?

At first we wandered around entranced by the huge bowls of spices, mountains of Turkish Delight, strings of necklaces, and racks of rugs and silk. But what should we buy? Standing in the middle of the hustle and bustle we held a quick conference. Julia was thinking big and wanted lamps and rugs and was prepared to ship them home if necessary. Clare and I were looking at small ornaments and Christmas presents. Sally wanted something to wear.

The waiting stallholders called out to us. If we showed the slightest interest in anything they would rush forward to talk, showing us more and more, luring us into the back of their shops and offering us tea so that we soon became a captive audience. We were excited but wary of being ripped off, while at the same time we were reluctant to pass up this experience. Fortunately Julia was a take-charge kind of gal.

"Let's decide how much we want to pay and stick to it – and remember we need to bargain here. We've got to haggle girls!"

"How *do* we haggle exactly?" I said uncertainly.

Sally said, "They'll start by giving you a high price and then you counter with something nearer to what you want to pay."

"And then, everyone sort of meets in the middle?" suggested Clare.

"And don't look as if you definitely want something – look sceptical," said Julia, pulling what she hoped was a sceptical, looking down her nose expression. "I vote we just dive in! I'm off to that rug shop!"

The rest of us followed behind her, giggling as we were ushered into the back room. We were seated around a low table while the shopkeeper brought out rug after rug to Julia. Sally brought out a calculator, and did some currency conversions. The rugs were all wildly expensive. Finally, Julia said, "I just want a small one. How much is that one?"

She was given a price. Julia looked carefully at the stitching and the fringing, pulling down the corners of her mouth.

"But this isn't a really fine rug," she complained.

Small glasses of tea were produced by the staff, and the rest of us pretended to look at rugs too. The price was reduced.

"I want it in red, actually," said Julia.

The shopkeeper and his sons went into action, unwrapping all kinds of red rugs. She chose one. A price was suggested. Julia looked at us. We all tried our best to look sceptical but how much lower would he go?

The shopkeeper read the room and asked us what else we were shopping for. Clare and I told him we had liked some intricately carved white trinket boxes at the entrance to the shop. The shopkeeper said they were made from meerschaum, a soft stone, and that Sir Arthur Conan Doyle wrote that Sherlock Holmes owned a meerschaum pipe. He showed us a pipe but although it was ornately carved, it was very expensive. The boxes, however, were reasonably priced. There was a pause. Then the shopkeeper said that the last price he quoted for the rug would now include two meerschaum boxes. Suddenly, we all looked happy. The deal was struck, and the parcel was wrapped.

"I think we've got the hang of it, girls!" said Sally when we got outside.

"Settle up with me later," said Julia triumphantly. "Next stop, Turkish Delight!"

Off (With) Your Trolley

Moyra Zaman

'My trolley was stolen in Tesco,' you cried,
and I laughed as I pictured you, standing tongue-tied!

... releasing your grip and scanning the shelves
for what should have been there, but was further along,
and turning to find that your trolley had gone!
It hadn't been moved and shunted nearby –
it was gone, mysteriously gone!

Bewildered, indignant, perplexed – what to do?
This behaviour, so out of the blue!
As an unseasoned shopper, quite taken aback
by this theft in broad daylight, a wounding attack,
you proceed to Enquiries to air your complaint.
You need help! What to do? What to do?

You seem like a child who's misplaced his mother,
depending on help in the hope to discover
the culprit, with trolley in tow.
The assistant proceeds to scan every aisle, asking
where you had left it and what it contained;
And progress seems tediously slow.

Then, in aisle number nine, you exclaim, 'That is mine!
– this poor trolley that must be retrieved.'
At first, you're relieved and then you're aware of
extraneous items sticking up in the air
on top of your shopping – how shocking it is,
this invasion of space – a disgrace, a disgrace!

You call the assistant to take them away;
and gripping your trolley, proceed on your way,
still eyeing the shoppers, suspecting them all
of diverting your items and ditching the haul.
You're still looking out for a possible thief
until you get home with a sense of relief.

I know that the next time you'll shop with a strategy
– a flag or a leash should be foolproof on Saturday!

Memories From The Seasons

Emma Barratt

This might seem strange but I do not really have a favourite season. I have favourite slices of every season.

I love warm sunny days on holiday by the sea when we have squeezed and wiggled into old wet suits and then plunged into freezing British seas to be buffeted by waves. Nothing really beats racing away over big waves on surging body boards. Your eyes sting, your mouth tastes of salt and the wave you are riding is so powerful that the adrenaline makes you think you are going to drown. I often laugh as I am deposited back on the beach; it makes me feel so alive.

In Polzeath they serve fresh pizza from an outdoor oven. After a morning in the cold sea and a perfect meal of cheesy, tomatoey deliciousness, exploring the delicate sea life in the surrounding pools is bliss. Those tiny microhabitats are fascinating at any age. I admire a crab's scuttling skills and a small flashing fish's ability to hide. Getting absorbed building sand monsters can be a whole day's entertainment. Redirecting beach streams with my son or building sea defences, makes me believe I could have been an engineer.

I love cold, icy, snow-laden mornings. I love the hush, the muffled quiet. I love how everyone is still in bed because there is no hope of getting to work. The anticipation of snowmen, sledging and snow angels makes me like an overexcited child. I have to get out in it. I love whizzing down hills and having a snowball fight. I have a glorious memory of my daughter in a bright blue snow suit, her hair flowing behind her as she swept head first down a hill on her bright red sledge, shrieking with laughter.

In every season I love the wind, the more untamed the better. The wind makes everyone skittish, flighty. Children laugh more, horses cavort and bolt. It's like a surge of electricity running through everything. It's particularly good by the coast during autumn, when the high winds turn the sea into ferocious works of art to be admired and respected.

The farm we lived on in Pennsylvania when I was nine had American beech trees growing around the clapboard house. I remember my mother sitting under them as my brother and I tore about trying to capture the golden treasure that twisted and danced in the wind. We had been told that catching leaves this way would bring us luck. We swept them up from the ground and threw them at each other too. We eventually collapsed on the ground next to my mum and she held us as the wind whipped round us. I felt so safe and happy.

I have a glorious memory of an Easter holiday at my grandparents' farm in Cumbria. Their home rested at the base of the great, grey, granite-topped hills that loomed up behind like swaggering giants. I remember endless warm early spring days, with soft winds, while my brother and I played in the nearby frolicking stream that ran over boulders and dark silt. We paddled in our wellies; mine were red and the water flowed over the top making them nice and squelchy. We searched under stones for creatures, we made little boats and climbed up the stream for hours exploring. I was only eight, and what I remember so clearly was the fun in the freedom. I also remember when one of the ponies escaped from the field, probably chased by the wind. I spotted her hoofprints in the mud. My grandmother praised my observation skills and I glowed warm with her praise.

My most recent memory comes from a walk I took up Ivinghoe Beacon in February. I sat in the car initially, listening to Radio 4 wondering if there would be any break in the rainy onslaught that was washing the car for me. The wind was strong enough to make the car rock from side to side! Eventually I decided I was going to have to go whatever the weather. I heard my grandmother's voice in my head: "You won't melt, darling!" so I pulled on my waterproof trousers and did my coat up to the neck. I pulled my hood up too. I put in my headphones and tucked my phone into the upper pocket. I have a playlist called COVID-19 and I listen to this when I am walking alone. It has a very eclectic mix; tunes to make me happy, sad or peaceful: Hank Williams, Elvis, Beverly Craven, Mozart, Taylor Swift, John Rutter and so on. Simply put, it allows me to feel things when I need to. Sometimes the music makes me cry, but that's OK because I let it. It helps me to let the sadness go.

Having decided to leave the warmth and safety of my car, I had to brace myself against the inside of it to be able to push the door open. I just stood and got used to the attack of the elements for a while after I got out. Eventually I fumbled for the play button on my phone, thanked the modern age that it was waterproof and started to walk gingerly down the path. The music that filled my ears was from the soundtrack of the movie *Il Postino*, which made me think of the glorious hot sunshine of the gulf of Naples and Sicily. All I could see in my mind's eye was the glittering white cliffs and sparkling blue seas. It made me laugh, with the contrast of the wind and rain that I was leaning into. I walked cautiously under the quivering oaks that border the path, their wet leaves occasionally blew onto me and stuck on my jacket. I looked like nature's version of a bedazzled nincompoop!

As I got halfway up the side of Ivinghoe Beacon I had to

stop to catch my breath and turned to look at the view. While I did so 'The Glory of Love' by Big Bill Broonzy started to play. It is so weird that this earth in the rain and wind seems like heaven. I could hardly see; a torrent of water was washing down my face and there I was singing along and dancing on the side of a vast chalk hill. It felt magnificent.

Later, on top of Ivinghoe Beacon 'I sat on the wind' with my arms spread wide and my face lifted to the stormy sky. 'We Can Win' by Rod Stewart started to play. It took me to Scotland but also gave me a rush of hope as the drums beat along to the sound of the rain. It is essentially a song about having faith. It seemed prophetic, it made me think that in all we are going through together, whatever our faith or beliefs are, we can cope. I suddenly felt lucky and grateful for what I have, so I did a little Scottish country jig in recognition.

I met only one other person that morning, the farmer. He was striding out in his jeans and a thin jacket, oblivious to the storm. I think he was checking on his sheep who were all cowering along the hedge trying to escape the cold and the wet. However, as we passed each other a thought crossed my mind that he might have been checking on the mad woman, dancing, by herself in the rain. Despite my strange appearance, he smiled. I could just about make out above my music and the whistling wind that he was wishing me a, "Good morning!"

I smiled back and called out, "Lovely morning!"

I think he must have realised I was OK.

Another Day

Lisbeth Cameron

Just under a year ago no one had heard about 'lockdown'. Today the whole world is engulfed in isolation, keeping distance, and shielding each other. The whole world is also wearing masks – just think about it – the whole world.

What could be so powerful, making such an impact? It is the virus COVID-19. We have the knowledge to fight this invisible enemy, and yet we need to know and learn more, but the impact is the same.

As a family we came home at the end of January 2020 after a holiday. We were full of energy and sold our two cars, replaced the garden gate, installed stairs into the attic – and then out of the blue it was lockdown.

Looking back, we had no idea how lucky we were to have done all that before everything stopped. We could not see friends or family. Thank goodness for today's IT and Zoom meetings: better than not seeing others at all.

We joined many people who used their time to do things they had wanted to do for a while – but that life did not give them time to do. Like tidying cupboards and drawers. Lockdown gave us an unusual special chance to do what had festered in the back of our minds for so long.

In early spring the garden got special care and a long beautiful, warm summer helped even more.

I spent more time reading books. I keep mine under the bed, so I can just reach down to make my choice. I got more time to play the piano, make jam and bake ryebread, which I had never tried before. We got even more time to join the neighbours for a Pimm's on the lawn.

What a beautiful summer it was. However, in the background one saw the soaring numbers: so many deaths in that area and so many in another. People desperate and out of work. Children creating havoc, not being able to go to school. The mental health difficulties of the nation added to a gloomy picture.

Why is the virus so infectious and why now? I think we should look at how little we do to take care of our globe, how we waste, pollute, and cut down nature for economic gain. I think that we have been destroying the environment and many species are extinct or in danger.

Maybe nature is fighting back? One impact of global warming is the loss of glaciers both on the North and South Poles. The warming of the seas is killing reefs and the micro-organisms which support the bottom of the food chain. It gets diseased. Bigger animals and fish get diseased. We get diseased and have no immunity. The world is screaming out for us to stop and think.

Are we intelligent enough to change our priorities and start to think about the consequences of our actions? We have to change and solve it here and now.

If not, we are all in it together and only have one globe to take care of; we are not able to go elsewhere.

Your Last Good Day

Richard Hounsfield

It's a wonderful thing, your Last Good Day,
you'll never know till it's gone;
we'll all have one sooner or later,
though we hope for more days in the sun.

A day arrived when harsh fate declared,
'We're atoning for sins from your past;
no mishaps or COVID but cancer for you,
the poker die have been cast.'

Millions have had this news that is bad,
the words that you don't want to hear,
'I'm sorry, dear sir, there's something down there,'
A dreaded lump that'll belt you with fear.

You wish you could go back to the second before
the moment the first cell went berserk,
but there's trillions of fate's moments already long gone
and changing some now cannot work.

So the mainsheet snaps and you're cast adrift,
waves of joy now become troughs of fear.
Nothing makes sense as the tears gouge away
your plan of living year after year.

The emotional 'coaster breaches right over,
you can't help the 'Why bloody me?'
Smoked, drank, too fat, genes, stress or just guess?
'Cursed injustice!' I cry angrily.

The leaving of loved ones and grandkids to come
is a pain hard to bear, I can't mask it;
all glittering dreams and sailing grand plans
flung from bucket list to stone cold casket.

Telling dear Mum, siblings, partner, chums,
and two lovely sons, 'I'm unwell,'
was the grief that I lived, my dread to inflict
this ride through a stormy sea swell.

Mad panic sets in, many jobs to get done,
how long have I got, how much time left to crank?
Yet you don't know the same as you didn't know before
Old Nick's drag to Death's Door swiftly turned to a yank.

The medics kick in, saviours fighting for you,
thumping scans, chemo spikes and X-rays.
Fortitude to fatigue, your health drains to pain,
fed through tubes, while your skin fries away.

Talk doctors, counsellors, family and mates,
good people hearing my rants, raves and tears,
helping my mind to the unravelling answer,
I'm going to have to face up to my fears.

Work elopes with the ego, a career's sailed away;
it's now legal deeds and financials to sum.
Problem one, chore two, three is a waste,
nag, quarrel and moan – why bother it's dumb.

Socrates said live an 'examined life',
be not swayed by frivolous matters.
You slowly resolve to forge a way forward,
finding value and meaning within tatters.

Your rudderless ship points and billows with sail,
the bashed hull finally gets underway;
the compass has moved as you're back in the groove,
'living' lest this is the Last Good Day.

Best to look forward with joy and good cheer,
laugh till your face turns to a crease.
Don't get bogged down in life's lottery draw,
soothe your mind with a new-found peace.

It's time to make hay, to sing dance and play,
find freedom, you yearn to feel real;
you've done your duty, now time for some "me!"
Catch the bits missed, pounding the life rat-wheel.

Writing and painting and anything creating,
the sun moon dogs birds, bees trees and sky sea.
You find your new eyes, and view stunning at Kew,
enjoy seeing old friends and adore family.

At gigs, pubs and clubs, where there's feasting on life,
you mimic those moments, 'cos that's what you do,
though worried and wondering if this is 'last call'
And if you can sustain what now used to be you.

When a bad day does come, it reminds you to smell
the roses and relish life when you're well.
As fatigue sets in and smiles are not easy,
Slow and stiff, is now the ashen death knell?

As your memory of you fades out of your view,
you look back on life with mixed faces,
asking yourself did you live each to the full?
You know for some, you weren't at the races.

But you had a good go, mistakes all in tow,
planting smiles on the dials of your crew,
and here you still are, better than hoped
fair fate held back, letting your soul renew.

Now walking the plank, sinking head out of bed,
Sweet Lord give me hope to carry on.
Your Last Good Day may be here today
but be thankful, you won't know 'til it's long gone.

ABOUT THE AUTHORS

(alphabetical)

Emma Barratt

Emma Barratt's main job has been as a full-time mum for nearly 21 years. She loves photography, art and music too but books, poetry and stories in all their forms fascinate her.

From the age of ten she has enjoyed writing diaries and letters. After university and a degree in Sociology she started a novel. Thirty years later she is still writing diaries and letters, and that novel!

Emma joined Linda Dawe's class at The White Hill Centre, Chesham about five years ago and has loved learning to write short stories and poetry. She has enjoyed getting to know the other group members and sharing her writing with them. It has made her happy. Throughout lockdown she has found that the group has been a wonderful support and inspiration and has led her to fall in love with writing all over again. She has found it an escape into the imagination and a joy.

Emma's contributions:

The Kitchen

The Storm

Star

Lessons From Chiltern Wandering

The Grey Cashmere Jumper

The Cupboard

Memories From The Seasons

Lisbeth Cameron

Lisbeth finds being a member of The White Hill Writers challenging, inspiring and, more especially, enjoyable.

She was born in Denmark but has lived in the UK for over 50 years. She began as a nurse, which included cycling through East London as a midwife. She has also been fortunate to have worked in many countries. Lisbeth has always written diaries, letters and articles. At school, her teacher said she wrote good essays. Now she mostly writes about life, mainly her autobiographical memories and her ideas about what is happening in the world. Occasionally they appear in poems or rhymes. She has published one book which was about her stay in the jungle of Guyana and is at present writing another about her early life. She writes songs for special occasions and her son and his newly wedded wife had to suffer one about their lives at their wedding reception.

Lisbeth's contributions:

A Look Through The Keyhole

Christmas Eve

The Beauty of Nature and Stillness

A Walk With Restorative Powers

Summer It Is

Another Day

Garry Giles

Garry Giles' first experience of creative writing was composing songs and their lyrics in the mid-1970s. He still writes songs today. Writing stories came much later as, with a busy career, time was not always available. Garry joined The White Hill Writers with the intention of writing a collection of short stories which is nearly complete.

Garry feels being part of the group has been a joyful journey, and given him the chance to learn from other writers, and along the way to produce more prose and poetry than he ever could have anticipated.

Garry's contributions:

The Clues

The Besuited Man

Oh Colourful You

I'm Being Swept Away

Up The Junction

Widower's Thoughts

In The Chilterns

Richard Hounsfield

Richard spent most of his career in front of software clients or behind a desk creating spreadsheets and legal documents as a Finance Director. Due to a life-changing event in 2018, he's exchanged those necessary duties for creative pastimes, i.e. painting, pandemic-inspired gardening, mindfully walking the dog and writing for pleasure.

Richard discovered The White Hill Writers in 2020, who have been incredibly welcoming, and motivated Richard to explore whether 'creative writing' was possible after churning out so many dry commercial documents over the years.

Richard also enjoys cricket, football, Formula 1, live music and motorbikes. He and his partner have just about survived raising their now grown-up children as a mixed step-family, plus their adorable golden retriever dog named Senna.

Richard's contributions:

Hurtling Terror

I Don't Know You...Don't I?

The Whimsical Wood

Bloody Butter Beans

The Kitchen Champ

You Used To Be Funny

Your Last Good Day

Sarah-Jane Reeve

Sarah-Jane began her career in the publishing world working on film magazines, before moving on to book promotion, editorial, production and retail. She has been a publishing freelancer for many years.

Sarah enjoys writing creatively and has contributed to anthologies such as *On Reflection* and *When This is All Over*. She is planning a book on the lives of her grandparents during the 1930s and 1940s which included numerous overseas postings. She is an enthusiastic gardener and traveller, and now lives in Berkshire with her husband and two daughters.

Sarah's contributions:

The Prisoner

1:30 am

A Midsummer Dream

Chiltern Walks

The River

Don't Forget Us

The Shopping Trip

Joyce Smith

Joyce has always enjoyed reading and after completing a degree at London University in History as a mature student, she started writing poetry and short stories. On retiring from the library service, she joined The White Hill Writers which enabled her to widen her scope and extend her skills.

Joyce also enjoys sketching and gardening, walking and swimming. She lives in Buckinghamshire near her three children and four grandchildren.

Joyce's contributions:

Ahmed

Amir

The Woman On The Bus

Autumn

The Butterfly

Vanilla Or Chocolate?

Another Time

Kate Stanley

Kate has lived in the Chilterns since the age of twelve, with the exception of three years in South Africa. Until recently she was a teacher and has been a carer for her husband for 25 years. Juggling the two roles was challenging but writing became her therapeutic outlet and she discovered The White Hill Writers in 2018.

Kate likes to write short, reflective pieces with the occasional foray into light-hearted verse. She has no plans to write a novel, preferring essays, articles and more recently an autobiographical blog.

Kate's contributions:

The Escape

Out Of The Darkness

An Eye On The World

Lunar Reflections

A Random Dash Through The Chilterns

Under Pressure

Lorraine Surridge

Lorraine recently retired after a career that spanned financial services, high street retail and local government. She is now enjoying spending time on more creative pursuits such as gardening and writing.

Since joining The White Hill Writers in 2018 she has been developing her writing style and she particularly enjoys writing historical fiction. Lorraine lives in Buckinghamshire and is married with one son.

Lorraine's contributions:

Kitchen Calamity

The Arrest

The Doorbell

Hunt The Rainbow

A Hole In The Fence

A Different Place

Step Back In Time

Moyra Zaman

Moyra, born in Glasgow, spent much of her life travelling and volunteering abroad and has always had an interest in dance and writing. Originally a research Biochemist she later trained in Fine Art and Textile Design. After working as a Colour Consultant for the Interior Design Market in London, she taught Art at Chesham Grammar School for 20 years. As International Coordinator she promoted Global Education, gained the International School Award, led World Challenge expeditions and developed a partnership in Ghana.

Now retired, she is a volunteer and trustee of the Workaid charity, teaches yoga and writes whenever she can. She lives in Amersham and is married with two sons and two grandsons.

Moyra's contributions:

The Intrusion

Snowfall

Looking At The Moon

The Wardrobe Lockdown

The Chilterns On My Doorstep

Lockdown Moments

Off (With) Your Trolley

Printed in Great Britain
by Amazon